JUSTICE
WEST OF
THE PECOS

Nick Castanis

American Literary Press
Five Star Special Edition
Baltimore, Maryland

Justice West of the Pecos

Library of Congress
Cataloging-in-Publication Data
ISBN-13: 978-1-56167-972-0

Library of Congress Card Catalog Number:
2007901452

Published by

American Literary Press
Five Star Special Edition
8019 Belair Road, Suite 10
Baltimore, Maryland 21236

Manufactured in the United States of America

Dedicated to my wife, Sarah, who encourages me to write, and write, and write . . .

1

It was unduly hot and dry in the early fall of 1876 as Elliot Stewart, accompanied by his companion, Rafer Summers, rode between towns in the vain effort of obtaining honest work.

Ex-confederate soldiers found employment and decent wages lacking in west Texas, even ten years after the bloody conflict. While honest men were merely attempting to survive, others resorted to a life of pillaging and thievery as law and order were struggling to be established. To the bandits, life was very cheap after battling in the gory insurrection.

Elliot's dark brown, unkempt hair and beard belied his thirty years, though hard wrinkles furrowed his otherwise handsome features. He was tall, rangy, and usually sat ramrod straight in the stirrups, Montana style, but soreness and tiredness had taken its toll, and he slouched to relieve the nagging back pain. He and Rafer were both proud Texans, having served with distinction with John B. Hoods' Texas Brigade. The devastation of General McClellan's federal legions in the infamous cornfield slaughter at Antietam in Maryland of 1862 awarded them a distinction not soon forgotten by veterans of both armies. It was at Burnside Bridge, same battle, that Rafer had stopped a federal miniball, giving him a permanent limp.

Rafer was smaller than Elliot, and although his black hair was shorter, his thick mustache was far more pronounced. The crows' feet spreading outward from the corners of his brown eyes were testimony to the frequency of his smiles.

Both men had dark, leathery skin from weeks spent in the unrelenting sun. After being mustered out together, the two had become inseparable friends.

They had departed Sonora two days earlier, where a temporary job had netted them only a little money for food. Their clothes were almost threadbare due to excessive wear and hard lye soap. Their long Johns were in worse condition. They did little for hygienic appearances, but at present, the two had no choice. Several days of riding would soon bring them to Fort Stockton, and they thought that their fortunes might reverse should labor be found.

"Dammit," Rafer said, "I'm dogged tired of eating rattlesnakes and jack rabbits. I got to get me some real vittles."

Elliot winced, saddle sore, and turned to him. "Rafe, old partner, I'm hungry too, so don't waste your talk on me. I sure could use a big steak, a nice cold bath, and some new duds, and a nice soft bed to sleep in — for a week."

Rafer laughed. "Yeah," he replied. "A real bed. Hell, I ain't slept in a real bed in, Lord, I don't know when. Some decent food to fill my belly, a shave, a bath, and oh yeah, a whore, too. I could use a whore, can't you?"

Elliot smiled and nodded affirmatively. "And this damned saddle is going to fall apart unless I can get it fixed real soon."

"We could've got it fixed," Rafer commented, "if I hadn't called that hombre in that Sonora saloon.

Me with a pair of aces and then he comes up with three deuces."

"I'm tired of you bringing that up," Elliot said, "so drop it, will you."

"But I was so sure that nobody could've beat them two aces, Elliot. That's why I bet all of my grub money."

Turning in the saddle to look at Rafter, Elliot countered, "Yeah, but some of that money was mine, too, or did you forget?"

Rafer looked down and murmured something incoherent.

"So," he said, changing the subject, "When do you figure we'll reach the Pecos?"

"I think maybe by sunup tomorrow," Elliot said, shifting uncomfortably in the saddle.

Scanning the shimmering horizon, Rafer continued, "You think we might run into some Injuns?"

"There's Indians everywhere, Rafe. We just been lucky we ain't run into some bad ones yet. Them Navajos is peaceable enough but them Shoshone can get nasty."

"What about them Comanches?" Rafer asked.

"Oh, now they can be really nasty, partner, but I don't reckon Comanches will be found this far north. Still, they move around a lot. Just in case we run into Comanche, Rafe, we don't stick around. I don't aim to tangle with them horse soldiers."

"Yeah," Rafer said, scratching inside his sweat-soaked shirt. "Why you suppose they call them horse soldiers anyway?"

"From what I've heard, they was born on a horse, they sleep and fight on a horse, they more'n likely suckle a horse and eat horse."

Rafer laughed aloud. It was not like Elliot to make jokes, but when he did, Rafer enjoyed it.

The broiling sun was reddening as it dropped toward the horizon. Dusk was near and dark came quickly on the plains.

Dismounting slowly, they pulled off their bedrolls, and uncinched the tired animals. Elliot rubbed his mare's back briskly, knowing that his weight had been borne on her all day. After hobbling their mounts, Rafer started a small mesquite fire as the night cooled rapidly. The sparse hardtack they consumed did little to relieve the grumbling in their stomachs.

Rafer wasted little time in going to sleep while Elliot sat up and stared into the fire. His thoughts soon turned to the terrible war that had changed so many lives. General Robert E. Lee's army, outnumbered, having failed to reach Hagerstown, Pennsylvania, after Antietam, was forced to retire southward. Both armies pulled away from each other to lick their wounds. Bivouacking that evening had allowed the mail to catch up. He still had the letter that he received from his 'intended' and pulled out the yellowed, damp letter and read it again. He knew the contents by heart. It began with the usual hatred of the war, the rationing of food, the missing mutual friends from Dallas they grew up with, the faltering confederate money, and the pitiful returning injured. Then, the letter took a turn. Elliot had been absent for so long and as she hadn't heard from him, Mary Louise presumed he had been killed. He had sent many letters to her, but obviously his latest ones never reached her. It was too late, as Mary Louise had met a Confederate major, fell in love, and gotten married. It ended with a sentence that read she did not believe her letter would reach him as she thought him dead, but, in case it did ...

Dead? He might as well have been dead now. She couldn't wait, could she? No, she had to fall in love with an officer while he was a lowly private. That major probably never left Dallas or never tasted action while he was constantly dodging miniballs and cannon grapeshot.

Disgusted, he crumpled the letter, hesitated, then threw it into the glowing embers, staring at it until it turned brown and burned.

Rafer snorted and turned over.

Elliot's thoughts turned to his family. His mother had died at his birth. His father had told him often enough that she had been a frail, but devoted mate. She was unable to cope with the hard rigors of life. His father, on the other hand, had been a big, tall man who worked on the railroad until his death, six years ago. Elliot's older sister had married and moved to Tyler, in east Texas, and he had not seen her nor met her husband in almost thirteen years. She probably had children and he might be an Uncle.

As he laid down and pulled the thin blanket under his chin, he heard Rafer snoring. He smiled and cocked his damp, seamy hat low over his eyes and finally fell asleep. During the night, the shrill howl of a distant coyote woke him momentarily but his tired eyes rolled back under his eyelids.

Late the following morning, he and Rafe reached the banks of the Pecos River. After stripping off their clothes, they romped in the cool, soothing water. Then, using a bar of hard lye soap, they bathed. Refreshed, they washed their filthy clothes, hanging them on a mesquite bush to dry. Later, Elliot dressed, and putting on his bolero, shouldered his rifle and walked along the bank. As he crossed a crest, he spotted an unsuspecting runt peccary rooting in the dirt. He fired and dropped him.

Rafer laughed and rubbed his hands when he saw Elliot returning with the pig-like animal. "Swamdoogle," he exclaimed, "We get to eat pork for a change. Give that thing to me and I'll skin him up."

"Put your duds on first, partner," Elliot replied. "I don't hanker you cooking my dinner in the raw."

It took a long time to roast the peccary, but the sweet smell was worth the wait. Then they both fell upon the blackened carcass and gorged themselves. After drinking heartily from the river, they lay back, sucking their teeth. Elliot rolled a cigarette and lit up, using a burning ember from the fire. "Lord, that was dee-licious," Rafer said.

"Uh-huh," Elliot retorted. "I feel a whole lot better."

"Do you feel sorry about leaving Dallas?" Rafer asked.

"Hell, man, there wasn't nothing in Dallas to keep us there."

"No, I guess not. It sure was a mite crowded and seemed that those Yankee carpetbaggers was taking over anyways. But, you miss Mary Louise, don't you?" Rafer said, looking at him.

Elliot was silent.

Rafer felt he had better drop the matter and as he reached for his tobacco pouch, a shadow fell across his face and he jerked upright.

The sun was behind the dark outline, but he immediately knew it was an Indian. He stood immobile and the Indian was joined by a second, and then a third.

"Easy, Rafe," Elliot cautioned, "easy. They got the drop on us, so don't make no sudden moves."

Elliot stood up and faced the intruders. At least the three didn't carry firearms, though their spears and bone handled knives were menacing enough.

Elliot raised his hand, palm toward the Indians. Likewise, they returned the peaceable gesture. The eldest Indian stepped forward.

"We are Navajo, white eyes. Do you know Navajo people?"

"Yes, we do," Elliot replied, "and we know the Navajo to be peaceful."

"Yes, we come in peace," the Indian said, looking around. "No other white eyes with you?"

"No, we are alone," Elliot said.

Nodding, the Indian continued. "We come long way from south and we are hungry. You have food for us to eat?"

"Why sure," Rafer said. "We got food. Come on down. You're welcome to what's left, chief."

"Me not chief, little one, but we eat, yes."

Slowly, the three approached them. Rafer pointed to the peccary's remains as they squatted around the fire. Tearing the creature apart, they stuffed their mouths and grunted frequently. Elliot and Rafer watched as the Indians ravished the meat and sucked on the bones.

When they had finished, Elliot said, "We're heading toward Fort Stockton, looking for work."

"Yes," the elder Indian replied. "We go Fort Stockton, too. You want we go all of us?"

"You mean together?" Elliot said. "Why, sure, that's all right with us. What are you called?"

"I am Mostaganuk Strong Arm — and you?"

'I'm called Elliot, and this here's Rafer, Strong Arm. I'm glad to know you. " He extended his hand, which was readily clasped by the Indian.

Elliot's hand returned greasy but he did not wipe it on his pants as it might offend the Indian. It was obvious to Elliot the other two were unable to converse with him and remained silent. At least they were not sullen.

The Indians unclothed and headed for the river. Rafer was glad they were not hostile and laughed aloud as the younger braves splashed water at each other. They were like children everywhere.

Later, Strong Arm talked of the plight of his family and race. The war had only slowed down the belligerence of the white man's hate for the red man. He had lost his wife and sons to renegades but held no animosity. He was just resigned to his fate, whatever comes.

Elliot felt sorry for these beleaguered people. He offered Strong Arm a smoke, who appeared appreciative at this gesture.

At dawn the next day, the five of them resumed their trek northward. The Indians slouched bareback on their mangy ponies, but kept pace. Elliot felt good, his stomach was full and his body somewhat cleaned, He attempted to keep ahead of the Indians, as the odor from their unwashed bodies nauseated him.

For two days they rode, and on the morning of the third, Elliot spotted several riders coming toward them. He looked at Rafer, who unsheathed his rifle and laid it across his lap. Their companions stopped, eyeing the oncoming riders closely. Elliot disengaged the rawhide tie-down from his navy Colt and he, too, reined up.

He counted four men in all. They were a rough looking bunch, but so were they. The four slowed their pace as they approached Elliot's group. Sizing them up quickly, Elliot noticed that the one in the lead was a large, grizzly looking man who squinted his eyes when scanning them. Elliot needed to watch him closely.

"Howdy," Elliot said. "You fellas coming from Fort Stockton?" He tried to be cheerful as one was never sure of strangers in this kind of country. The man, with tobacco spittle, brown and fresh, coursing the corners of his mouth, stopped his mount. Leaning forward, his eyes narrowed under the shadow of a wide brimmed hat pulled tightly over his forehead.

Elliot, uneasy, waited for an answer. He noticed that the hombre immediately following the big man began to smile. He was leaner and sported a huge, unkempt beard. A trigger tied six-shooter was nestled in his belt and his hand was never far from it.

"What're you boys doing with them Injuns?" the big man said.

"Hell," Rafer replied, "we're just traveling together. Why?"

"I don't cotton to Injuns myself, and neither do my friends here, stranger."

"Mister," Elliot said, "they don't mean no harm to nobody. So if you don't mind, we'll just keep moseying on."

Spitting, the man said, "You're a Johnny Reb, ain't you, boy?"

"Yep, used to be, but that was a long time ago, mister. Now, if you just let us pass - ."

"I'll tell you when you can get by me, Reb," said the man, wiping his mouth.

The Indians were getting nervous as they looked at one another. Although they might not readily understand the language, they could surmise the situation by facial and body expressions.

Elliot did not want a useless confrontation, but the stranger and his companions were blocking their way. His jaw now set, he said, "Just what is it you want, Mister?"

The stranger smiled and quickly drew his gun. Elliot watched as he shot one of the Indians, who groaned and fell off his pony.

"That's what I wanted," laughed the man, turning to his companions. "A good Injun is a dead Injun, ain't it, fellas? Now, Reb, you got something to say about it?"

"You had no call to do that, mister," Rafer said angrily. "He wasn't gonna give you no trouble."

The antagonist, glaring at Rafer, recocked his pistol and waved it in his direction. That move was all Elliot needed as he spurred his horse while whipping out his pistol. The bully's horse shied as Elliot's mare ran into it. This momentarily surprised the man as Elliot's pistol barked. The slug caught the man high on the left shoulder and off-balance, he toppled backward. Falling on his head, the man's huge bulk jackknifed his neck. He lay still.

The others quickly raised their hands, not wanting to challenge Elliot.

"You," Elliot demanded of the full-bearded one, "get down and see to him. I just hit him in the shoulder." Dismounting, the man rolled the big one over. In a moment, he looked up.

"His neck's broke. He's dead."

"Hell, boys, Elliot didn't mean to kill him, did you, Elliot?" Rafer said. "No, but it's done, partner," Elliot said nervously. "I can't undo it. The rest of you fellas dismount and get rid of your bully friend after we're gone. Just what was his name anyway?"

"That was Big Jim Murtaugh you just killed, stranger," said the bearded man.

"Hell, I didn't kill him, dammit. The fall did," Elliot exclaimed. "Strong Arm, check your friend."

The wounded Indian struggled to get up with the help of Strong Arm. Remounting, the Indian was bleeding from a wound in his side.

"That Murtaugh," Elliot said, "He any kin to either one of you?"

"No sir, he ain't," replied the bearded man, "but he has a twin brother up Las Cruces way, I hear."

"Well, the dead man's got no use for his horse, so Strong Arm, you take him for your troubles. Any objections, fellas?" Elliot said, trying to still the agitated Toter.

The men shook their heads in unison.

Elliot bolstered his weapon and then said, "Let's move out of here."

As they rode away, Rafer said, "Elliot, you ain't one to aim for a man's shoulder. You should've gut shot him outright."

"I ain't proud of what happened, Rafer. Not one bit," Elliot commented.

About a mile down the road, the Indian, Strong Arm, halted his pony and the others followed suit.

"What's the matter, Strong Arm?" Elliot asked, halting his mount and looking back.

"You good man," the Indian said, "but we not be with you no more. White men give you much trouble if we go together - you savvy?"

"I understand," Elliot replied. "You are a friend, so go in peace."

He and Rafer watched as the trio turned and rode away.

Elliot reached down and rubbed his mare's neck. She had been a grand companion to him for three years. He had named her Toter because she had never shied from carrying his bulk.

"Well, they almost lost that Indian buck, but they gained a horse anyways," Rafer said. "Some trade, huh?"

2

ort Stockton was a small, dusty village, with the main street bordered on both sides by clapboard sided stores — a saloon, two livery stables, with a blacksmithy under a lean-to near one, and a two-story hotel in the middle. The hotel was directly across the dirt street from the saloon. It was near noon, and Elliot and Rafer noticed only a few people milling about. A couple of cowhands stared at the dusty men as they slowly made their way down the street.

They pulled up in front of the saloon and dismounted. Hitching his horse, Elliot stretched to relieve his soreness. As he looked around, he was disappointed as he figured that this small, one-horse village offered little chance for work.

"Elliot, we got any money left?" Rafer asked.

"Damned little, Rafe, why?"

"I sure would like a drink of whiskey," Rafer said, rubbing his mouth and chin.

"Okay, maybe we can afford one apiece, partner, but just one, you hear?"

The saloon was dim as they first stepped in, the flickering wall lamps casting eerie shadows in all directions. There were several men standing at the bar who glanced casually their way, then resumed their drinking and talk. Elliot and Rafer each ordered a shot of whiskey. Elliot sipped his slowly and winced as the liquor burned his throat. Still, cheap though it was, the whiskey was appreciated.

He heard Spanish being spoken behind him, and turning slowly, he saw a tall Mexican standing by a table across the room. Directly below the tall Mexican sat an immaculately attired Mexican gentleman, apparently reeking of noble birth. His black pants were stitched down the side with gold thread and flared at the bottom. His bolero sparkled of gold colored sequins, tightly woven into the elegant material. The gentleman was elderly, but his white hair was full and finely groomed. His features were delicate.

The younger Mexican seemed to be guarding him.

After a few moments, the seated Mexican looked up and noticed that Elliot was staring at him.

"Gentlemen," he said, gesturing with his hand, "please, one moment of your time."

Elliot, drink in hand, walked over, followed by Rafer.

The elderly Mexican stood up and offered his hand. "Gentlemen, you are strangers to Fort Stockton, are you not?" This man spoke better English than he did, Elliot thought.

Elliot took the man's hand and shook it. "Yes sir, we are," he replied.

"My name is Emilio Santiago De Paolo, amigos."

"My name is Elliot Stewart, sir, and this here's my partner, Rafer Summers. I'm glad to make your acquaintance."

"Forgive me, senors, but are you hungry?"

"We sure are, mister," Rafer replied.

"Then, please, be my guests and eat what you will here," the Mexican said, spreading his hands outward at the food displayed on the table.

Rafer started to grab at the food, but Elliot stopped him. "What's the catch, senor?"

"Catch? Senor, I do not understand what you mean?"

"People don't just give away something for nothing, senor," Elliot said.

"Oh, I see," the gentleman replied. "Yes, there is no catch, as you say. But first you eat, then we talk. The food and whiskey will cost you nothing, amigos. Please, help yourselves."

Now released, Rafer grabbed at the pone cakes, the boiled eggs, and beef slices. Stuffing his mouth full, Rafer's eyes were dancing gleefully. The gentleman picked up a whiskey bottle and refilled their glasses. Elliot, although puzzled, decided that as long as the food and drink were free, he might as well take advantage of it.

The food, filling Elliot's stomach quickly, somewhat nauseated him, but he didn't stop as satisfying his hunger was paramount. After finishing, he wiped his mouth with his sleeve and turned again to the smiling Mexican.

"Thank you, senor," he said gratefully. "Now what is it you want to talk about?"

"Amigos, I am looking to hire a few good vaqueros, or as you say, cowboys, to drive some horses to my ranchero in New Mexico. If the two of you are interested, I will pay you well," the gentleman said.

"Where in New Mexico?" Elliot asked.

"It is quite near Las Cruces, senor."

"Hmm, that means we go through El Paso, don't it?" Elliot asked.

"Yes, amigo. Should you decide to join us, my foreman here will guide you. Oh, forgive me, amigos, I forgot my manners. This is Chavez Ramon. Not only is he my foreman but my trusted companion as well."

Elliot looked at the unsmiling, burly foreman. He was not a typical Mexican, being very tall, taller than Elliot. His black hair was not long, yet his graying sideburns reached and tucked under his jawbones.

A stoic expression meant that he would brook little nonsense from anyone.

Turning back to Paolo, Elliot said, "Well, Senor Paolo, just how many hands you got signed up so far?"

"Only two at this moment, my friend, but I require five in all."

"How many horses are you moving, sir?" Elliot inquired, watching Paolo light up a thin cigar.

"There are fifty in all, gentlemen," he said. "Would you care for a cigar?"

"No thanks. But why do you need six riders for only fifty horses, sir? Surely, they're broke, ain't they?"

"But, of course, Senor Stewart."

"What's the pay, senor?" Rafer asked.

"Gentlemen," Paolo said, smiling, "I am prepared to pay each of you sixty dollars in gold."

"In gold?" Rafer cried. "Elliot, he said sixty dollars in gold."

"I heard him, Rafe."

"Yes, amigos, ten dollars at this moment and fifty upon the safe delivery of the herd," Paolo exclaimed.

Elliot, puzzled, figured there had to be more to this than met the eye. Rafer tugged at his sleeve.

"Senor, would you excuse us for a minute," Elliot said. "We would like to talk it over." He pulled Rafer aside. "Partner, this is kind of hard to believe. Sixty dollars seems awfully high just to deliver fifty horses, and broken in horses at that. Must be something here I don't understand."

"Who cares, Elliot," Rafer replied. "The man said sixty dollars in gold. Why, that's four months wages on any ranch for a hundred miles. Where else we gonna get that kind of money, tell me that? I'm all for taking the job."

"Well," Elliot continued, "then how come he ain't hired plenty of wranglers up to now for that price, tell me?"

"I'll tell you why, mister," interrupted an eavesdropper. Elliot turned to look at him as the man continued. "Do you know that you'll be traveling through Comanche territory?"

"Yeah," Elliot replied, staring at the stoop-shouldered interloper. "So what?"

"Mister, have you seen them horses that Mexican's got?"

"Hosses is hosses," Rafer said.

"Them horses ain't your regular horses, mister. They is a breed you ain't never seen before and like as not, never see again. And if them Comanche see them horses, your life ain't worth sixty cents, much less sixty dollars, and mister, that's the truth."

Turning to Elliot, Rafer said, "What kind of horses could they be anyway, Elliot?"

"I don't know, Rafe."

"Hell, partner, we been looking for a job for a long time now and I like to eat kind of regular," Rafer alluded, raising his whiskey to his mouth. Turning to the interrupter, Elliot said, "Thanks, mister, for your information. Let's go, Rafe."

Returning to the table, Elliot said, "We'll take the job, senor."

"Fine, fine," the Mexican replied. "Please to sign here, gentlemen."

As Elliot and Rafer signed the contract, the Mexican gestured to his foreman, who produced two new ten-dollar gold pieces from his bolero.

"Now that we have signed up to help deliver your horses," Elliot inquired, "would you tell us a little more about these special animals?"

The Mexican smiled. "Certainly. A few weeks past I found out about these horses. They had been brought here from a country called Arabia. They were shipped to Galveston, but the gentleman who brought them here was unable to pay for them due to money misfortunes. I bought them at auction and put them aboard a boat. They were shipped upriver to the Nueces River basin and from there to here. Unfortunately, the cowhands that brought them here squandered their money on drink and left,"

"Well, all I can say, sir, is that they must be some very special horses for you to go to all that trouble," Elliot declared.

"Amigo, I am a lover of good horse flesh, and these, let me say, are the finest in all the world," the Mexican said, "but you will see for yourselves."

Paolo took the gold pieces from his foreman and handed one each to Elliot and Rafer. "So, gentlemen, I must leave for Old Mexico, but Chavez will guide you as soon as we are fortunate enough to sign one more vaquero. Thank you both, and will you be staying at the hotel tonight?"

"I guess so," Elliot replied. "I need to get some saddle work done and some new duds too."

"Excellent," Paolo beamed, "then we see you tomorrow." They shook hands, and Elliot noticed that Paolo's hand was small and delicate, yet firm. He seemed like a sincere person.

As soon as Elliot and Rafer left the saloon, they walked their horses to the nearest livery stable. After instructing the owner to feed and board their ponies, Elliot asked him to repair his saddle. Then, draping their saddle bags over their shoulders, they retreated to the old hotel and registered. They were directed to a small room on the second floor, which contained one bed, two hardbacked chairs, and a vanity which had a china basin located beneath a weathered mirror. There was a pitcher of tepid water next to the basin. The single window was draped with tattered cheese cloth curtains.

Satisfied with the room, Elliot tossed his saddle bag in the corner. "Let's go get a shave now, partner."

"Sure, and maybe another drink too, huh?"

"Why not," Elliot said, smiling.

"And - and maybe a whore?" Rafer asked.

"Rafe. We ain't got that kind of money. Leastways not yet, anyway," Elliot said teasingly.

They entered a tonsorial parlor and got a shave and a hair trim. Then Elliot suggested that they take a much- needed bath to relax their aching bodies and get rid of the grime at the same time.

An aged Indian woman poured warm water over their heads, and when she turned for more, Rafer pinched her on her large rear. She giggled, trying to hide her gapped stained teeth. Rafer winked at her.

She wasn't much, but Rafer ached for a woman to relieve himself. Looking over, he noticed that Elliot was smiling at him.

"Well," Rafer said, "What're you looking at?"

Elliot laughed. "You're pitiful, Rafe."

After finishing, Elliot paid the owner and they returned to the saloon. Paolo and Chavez were gone. Elliot wondered if their absence meant they had found their remaining wrangler. Downing his whiskey, Rafer remarked how good it felt to be clean with his belly full.

"Well, Rafe," Elliot commented, "it's been a long day, and I'm tuckered out. I'm thinking about going to bed."

"I know what you mean, partner," Rafer exclaimed. "I been thinking about that bed, too. Let's go."

Sitting on the side of the bed taking his boots off, Elliot said, "I hope we did the right thing."

"Hell, Elliot, this is the best thing that's happened to us since we left Dallas. We got a little money, something to eat and a job. That's more'n we had in quite a spell. Well, ain't it?"

16

"Yeah, but I'm a little uneasy about all this," Elliot reflected. "Anyway, what's done is done." He laid down and before he dozed off, fantasized once again of the lovely Mary Louise.

They slept late the following morning, enjoying the softness of the mattress as long as they could. Eventually, however, noisy stomachs proclaimed the return of their hunger, so they dressed and went downstairs for breakfast. After consuming a hearty meal of flapjacks, bacon and eggs, they both leaned back and smoked.

"Lord, that was delicious," Rafer said as the smoke enveloped his head. Then he looked up and said, "Here comes the Mex."

Elliot turned and their eyes met. Amid the jangling of oversized spurs, the Mexican foreman, Chavez, approached them.

"Amigos," Chavez said, "I trust you slept well?"

Both nodded.

"Good, we leave this evening. You are to meet me at the stockyard north of town. Agreed?"

"Agreed," Elliot replied. "But why do we leave so late?"

Chavez looked around the room and then back to Elliot. 'It is my wish that we leave at a time of day that is free of many eyes, my friend."

"Huh?" Rafer grunted.

"I understand, Amigo," Elliot said.

Chavez turned and departed, leaving Elliot to wonder how anyone could walk straight with such unwieldy spurs.

That afternoon, Elliot and Rafer wandered over to the livery stable.

"Got your saddle fixed, mister," the stable owner said proudly.

Elliot scrutinized the repair work closely.

"Good job, huh?" the owner said.

"Not bad, not bad at all," Elliot replied. "How much we owe you?"

"Well, let's see. One dollar for the saddle, a dollar apiece for feed and rubdown, and one-half dollar each for keep. That comes to exactly four dollars, mister. That sound fair to y'all?"

"Fair enough, mister," Elliot replied, paying him.

They walked their horses over to the gunsmith, and after hitching their mounts, entered. They purchased a few cartridges for pistols and rifles. Then they went to the General Emporium and bought a new shirt and pants apiece.

"Well," Elliot said, "Partner, we are almost broke again."

"Yeah, but we sure got our money's worth. I just regret I never got me a whore. Now that would've made my whole day, Elliot."

Elliot laughed. "We got a little time to kill before we go to the stockyard, partner. So maybe we could get one more drink."

As they crossed the road, headed toward the saloon, they ran into Strong Arm. Rafer hailed the Indian, who slowly made his way toward them.

"I see white men look good this day," Strong Arm said. "You got money now?"

"Yeah," Rafer said. "We got a job herding some horses to New Mexico."

Strong Arm frowned. "Is that the ponies at the stockyard north of town, white man?"

"I suppose," Elliot replied. "We ain't seen them yet, but sure heard a lot about them."

"White man must go with care," the Indian warned. "The ponies are different and Comanche have good eyes." He pointed to the north. "The Apache will not attack many white men, but the Comanche not care and they will attack. You savvy?"

"Yes, we understand," Elliot replied.

The Indian continued. "Do not fight Comanche from horseback. Better you get off horse and shoot from ground. Comanche too good on horse."

"Thanks for the warning, friend," Elliot said as they continued on to the saloon.

"You believe what he said?" Rafer inquired.

"You mean about fighting from the ground? Sure, I do. It's much easier trying to draw a bead on a man while kneeling. Hell, Rafe, you know that."

"Yeah, I suppose so," Rafer said, uneasy.

That afternoon, there appeared to be more patrons in the saloon than yesterday. They ordered a shot glass of whiskey and sipped. Looking around, Elliot eyed five men sitting at a nearby table, playing poker. One man in particular, sporting a tall black hat, caught his attention. His card dealing acumen was slick, thought Elliot ~ too slick. He nudged Rafer, who turned to look.

Elliot leaned over and whispered in Rafer's ear. "Don't ever play cards with a man like that. He's too good. Look at his hands."

"Damn it, stranger," called out one man at the table, "how the hell did you come up with three queens when I discarded one and there's the other one ashowing?"

In a split second, the man with the tall hat jumped up, reaching inside his bolero, but before he could make another move, a pistol roared and a forty-four slug tore through his midriff. Doubling over, the man fell across the table and money flew everywhere.

"Damn," Rafer cried, "that hombre was fast."

"Yeah, he was," Elliot replied. "Drink up, Rafe, and let's make tracks out of here."

Elliot could have seen the confrontation taking place. The card shark was living on borrowed time. It was a wonder he had not been done in before this.

At dusk, the two slowly rode toward the stockyard, where they spotted Chavez sitting on a fence rail. Then they saw the horses. Elliot noticed that Toter perked her ears.

"Gawd amighty, Elliot," Rafer cried. "Look at them hosses. I ain't never seen critters like them before. Hell, if I was an Injun, I'd kill for just one of them things myself."

They both stared at the spirited horses in the enclosure. The animals had full flowing manes, with high withers and razor thin shanks. Most were white, while some had pale gray bodies and tails. Their dark eyes were clear and seemingly full of fire.

"Chavez, I can certainly appreciate your concern for these horses," Elliot said as he dismounted "They are beautiful, for a fact."

"True, amigo, they are beautiful, as you say," Chavez agreed.

"But they ain't as big as our quarter horses," Elliot said, peering through the fence rails.

"No, but they are strong and fast, amigo. Look at the big chests. They do not blow as hard as the quarter horses," Chavez remarked, as he jumped from the fence. "Come and meet the others."

There were several men squatting near a small fire as they approached.

"This is Senor Tom Travis, amigos," Chavez said.

When Tom raised up, Elliot stood next to a big man with a brown beard and a bald pate. Tobacco stain covered most of his facial hair, and his face was pockmarked with numerous blackheads, most likely due to the lack of applied soap or care. Elliot's immediate impression of this giant was that he could hold his own in a fistfight.

"Where you hail from, Tom?" He asked.

"Laredo. You been there?"

"Sure, there ain't many places in Texas I don't know," Elliot replied, extending his hand.

"And this one," Chavez continued, "is Senor Billy Carr. He is from New Orleans, yes?"

Billy nodded. He was lean, young and sported a tartan belted bowler, squared low on his head. Long dark hair spilled from the hat's rear brim, and Elliot noticed his holster slung low on his left thigh. His hands were small, but Elliot thought that he must be quick. The man smiled readily, though.

"And here is Senor Mitchell, amigos," Chavez said. "Please, I forget your first name."

"Devon, Devon Mitchell, mister, and what is your name?"

"I'm Elliot Stewart, fellas, and this here's my partner, Rafer Summers."

Devon was of medium height, with bushy red hair and a short mustache. He had a large frame and looked as if he could whip a pack of pumas. But he had a ready grin also and rose to shake Elliot's hand.

With the amenities concluded, Chavez forwarded directions as to the individual riding positions they each would take during the drive.

"Amigos, until I decide who will relieve me, I will take the point," Chavez said, looking each wrangler in the eye. "Now, we wait until dark so as not to disturb the townspeople when we leave. Then we will ride for two hours and stop for the night."

Elliot sauntered over to look at the horses again. Young Billy Carr accompanied him.

"You in the war, Mister Stewart?" Billy inquired, putting his foot on a lower rail.

"Yeah, me and Rafe both were," Elliot replied.

"Did you kill many Yankees, or do you feel like talking about it?" Billy asked.

"I saw too many good men die, Billy, on both sides. It wasn't no pretty sight, I'll tell you that."

"Your partner, Rafer, he got that limp in the war?" Billy said.

"Yeah."

"Them's pretty horses, ain't they," Billy said.

Elliot nodded.

Rafer walked over, holding two tin cups full of coffee. He handed one to Elliot and looked between the corral rails.

"Yessir," Rafer said, "Wouldn't surprise me if we get jumped by Indians before we're ten miles out."

"Does that bother you, Mister Summers?" Billy asked.

"Why sure it bothers me. Don't it bother you?"

"After running into all kinds of toughs in New Orleans, no, not really," Billy said, smiling. Elliot had him pegged right. This cocky kid wouldn't scare easily. But that remained to be seen for sure.

Travis walked over and looking Elliot up and down said, "Stewart, you any good with that hog leg?"

"Tolerable, but I prefer my rifle, Tom — why?"

"Well, if we meet up with Indians or Comancheros, I'd like to know who I can depend on."

"Mr. Travis", Rafer interrupted, "You ain't got to worry about me or Elliot. We've managed to keep our hair up to now. Hell, just the other day, some hombres stopped us and ..."

Elliot, perturbed at Rafe's outburst, leered at him. Rafe, seeing this, cut short his conversation,

"So, what happened?" Travis inquired.

"Nothing, nothing much. We just stared them down. Nobody got hurt", Rafer said, lying.

Travis grunted and turned away.

"He talks too much", Billy said, looking Tom's way.

"Yeah, and so does somebody else I know", Elliot said, glancing at Rafer.

"New Orleans, huh", Elliot said, quickly changing the subject. "I'll bet it's a big town." "Yep, sure is", Billy responded, "big and rich and just full of beautiful southern belles." "So, why'd you leave anyway?" Rafer asked. "Had to", Billy remarked. "Shot a man." "Did you kill him?" asked Rafer.

"Naw, but he was a big man in Orleans and I had to make tracks in a hurry." "What was he riled up about?" Rafer continued.

"His young daughter opened up to him that I took advantage of her, and I didn't. She came on to me and well, I just did what was natural." Everyone smiled.

"That Devon there", Billy commented, "now he ain't too bright, but he seems pleasant enough." "I hope so", Elliot said. "I'd hate to have to tangle with that one."

With the sun down, the drovers mounted their horses and quietly releasing the thoroughbreds, moved northward out of town with Chavez in the lead.

After a short trek, Chavez called a halt and dismounted. He asked Devon to take the first watch after supper, which consisted of bacon, beans, and strong coffee.

"Chavez," Elliot said, "your boss, he got a big spread?"

"Si, amigo, my Patron has near five leagues of land."

"Whew," Rafer said, whistling. "Five leagues is pretty near twenty thousand acres, ain't it, Elliot?"

"Damn good piece of land at that," Billy interjected.

"How come one man owns so much land?" Travis asked of Chavez.

"Years past, amigos, about two hundred years ago, a wise and fearless Conquistador by the name of Diego De Vargas opened this territory to our people. He tamed the savages here somewhat and proclaimed the land in the name of the Spanish king."

Billy, listening intently, poured himself another cup of coffee as Chavez continued.

"The king gave De Vargas the money and forces necessary for this, as you say, venture. My patron's wife, God rest her soul, was directly kin to De Vargas, and Senor Paolo, through marriage, received a land grant because of De Vargas' achievements."

Travis, placing another stick on the fire, spat tobacco juice into it and sat back down. Elliot found Chavez's story interesting and thought that with twenty thousand acres, this Paolo must be very rich.

22

'In forty-eight, I think," Chavez said, moving the sticks around in the fire, "when the Yankees took over this territory, the treaty of Guadalupe Hidalgo allowed Senora Paolo to retain her possessions."

"And just exactly where is this spread?" Billy asked.

"It lies near the Jornada Del Muerto mountains, north of Las Cruces, my friend. It is a very beautiful place, and my Patron has a wondrous hacienda there. But you will see,"

Elliot, rolled a cigarette. "Chavez, I've heard a lot about the Lincoln County Wars going on in New Mexico. You people involved with that?"

"No, amigo, thankfully. That war is bad, very bad, but we are fortunate that it is in the north."

"Well, what about Indians?"

"Si, we have savages, but they are everywhere. Once in awhile they come to our range and kill a steer or two, but we do not harbor a grievance toward them. You must understand, amigos, some are starving and are in need of food. After all, it is we who are the true transgressors."

Rafer leaned toward Elliot and whispered, "What's that there word?" Elliot waved him off.

Travis stood up, and stretching, said that he was going to get some sleep as he had to relieve Devon before daylight.

"There is a Mescalero Apache reservation that borders our range," Chavez said, lighting a cigar, "but they do not give us much trouble. They leave us alone and we leave them alone. It is the Comanche that are troublesome and the half-breed Comancheros are worse. The Comanche are superb horsemen and fierce warriors. Even other tribes try to avoid them."

"I heard," Elliot said, "that it is best not to try to fight them from horseback. Any truth to that?"

"Yes, it would be best, amigo. Even the yellow legs, the calvary soldiers, do not desire to fight the Comanche from horseback."

"I sure don't want to mess with them," Rafer said nervously, fanning out his bedroll.

"Hell, boys," Billy chimed in, "they'll drop just as well as the next man. If I can see them, I can drop them." He patted his holster.

Elliot hoped that it wouldn't come to that, but this country had to be crawling with Indians.

"Hey, Chavez," Rafer said, "about how many steers ya'll got on your range?"

"We have many, amigo, perhaps four thousand, perhaps more. We will have a better count come next spring."

The fire was beginning to die down and the night chill crept in.

"Will Mister Paolo be hiring on more permanent hands soon?" Rafer inquired.

"Perhaps, amigo, perhaps," Chavez said.

"What's the best way to get to the ranch from here, Chavez?" Billy asked.

'It is best that we avoid the Guadalupe Mountains, so we must go through El Paso, hopefully at night, then we travel north keeping the Rio Grande to our left. But that is enough, amigos, for this night. We have a long way to go tomorrow, and we start early."

The small fire was now glowing embers as Elliot spread out his bedroll and lay down. He stirred only when Chavez awoke Travis to relieve Devon on watch.

3

As the group resumed their trek the next morning, Elliot was elated that at present he was not riding drag. Poor Tom Travis must be eating more of his share of dust following the horses, and as the day grew increasingly hotter, it would be more uncomfortable. At least the spirited horses behaved well, but the hands kept them tightly bunched as a precaution. One black stallion in particular caught Elliot's eye. He would love to trade in his beat mare for that one. He wondered how much a horse like that would cost. The horse had great lines, with a large chest and white marked hooves ~ a beautiful animal, indeed.

As the day wore on, rivulets of sweat meandered down the nape of Elliot's neck until his checkered bandana was soaked. Dust powdered him and his mare. The slow pace reminded him of the marches between battles a decade ago, though the lush greenery of the Shenandoah Valley of Virginia and Pennsylvania was a far cry from the arid basins of Texas. Ofttimes, however, those marches and battles produced a thirst that was impossible to quench. But rains were certainly more timely and frequent there than in west Texas, sometimes producing impassable quagmires. Hard enough to fight when one was already tired of tramping in mud for days on end. How even the wildflowers survived in this dry country was akin to a miracle.

Looking ahead, he watched as Chavez frequently turned in the saddle to check the horses and riders. He appeared to be completely devoted to Paolo. Chavez's huge sombrero bounced ungainly on his head but he rode a magnificent horse.

That evening, the men huddled around the campfire, sipping coffee. Elliot, seated, stared at the embers, his mind wandering back and forth between daydreams and the present. His eyes were half-closed when he heard Billy talking to Rafer.

"Where did you get wounded, friend?" Billy inquired.

"Place called Burnside Bridge at Antietam," Rafer said. "Ever heard of it?"

"Yeah, I heard of it. Lots of men died in that battle, I was too young to join up, but I would have, had I had the chance," Billy remarked.

"Thank your stars you didn't, Billy. It ain't grand, I can tell you that. It's something you don't want to see."

"You Rebs never knew when you was licked, did you?" Travis said, laughing.

"Shut your greasy face," Billy said.

Travis, glaring at him, slowly rose and spit into the fire. He expanded his chest, apparently challenging young Billy.

"Don't get any ideas," Billy said calmly. "You make the wrong move, man, and I'll kill you where you stand." His left hand moved down his side. They stared at one another for a brief moment.

Taking the edge off the affair, Chavez jumped up. "Gentlemen, please, remember why we are here. I need each one of you to finish this drive."

"Yeah, Travis," Elliot said. "Relax, no harm done. Here, have some more coffee." He poured Travis a fresh cup as tensions eased.

"So," Billy continued, "you and Elliot then came back to Texas, huh?"

"Yeah," Rafer replied. "It took us awhile. We didn't have no horses and had to beg people with wagons for a ride. Back in Dallas things was a mess for a long time. Got me a job sweeping in a warehouse Got me a girlfriend, too. But as I didn't have no money, she took up with a Yankee soldier and that was that." He sighed. "So, me and

Elliot decided to move on."

"What do you say we call it a night", Elliot remarked. "I'm bushed."

Silently, the men moved away from the fire while Chavez kicked sand on the embers.

The next day was a repetition of the one before. The oppressive heat, however, seemed to come earlier. Elliot mused that this godforsaken country was only good for gila monsters and sidewinders, certainly not made for white men. Again he thought of Mary Louise, her pure, white perfumed skin and flighty, talkative manners. Lord, he had loved that girl. Damn the war that separated them and finally cost him a wife. But what choice did he have? He had to go to war. Texans, because of the heavy tax burdened on them for cotton destined overseas, could ill have afforded to allow Congress to continue this unwarranted penalty. The slave issue was of secondary importance. Had South Carolina not initiated the conflict, Texas most likely would have, Elliot thought.

Around noon, he spotted a lone rider approaching, heading straight for Chavez. With these expensive, unusual animals in tow, he did not welcome strangers, but perhaps the man knew Chavez.

The stranger reined up parallel to the Mexican and began talking. Occasionally, he turned in his saddle and glanced at the horses. He must be impressed by them, Elliot thought, but who wouldn't be?

After a few minutes, the man left, but he was heading back in the direction he just came from ~ El Paso. He didn't look Mexican, but at this distance, Elliot couldn't tell.

Chavez, still on point, turned, and seeing Elliot, motioned for him to come forward. Elliot spurred his mount and slowed up next to Chavez.

"Amigo," Chavez said, "have Travis come to me, and you take his place, quickly "

Without a word, Elliot turned and galloped to the rear, passing the message to Tom, who in turn rushed forward after pulling his bandana off his face. After a brief discussion, Travis left Chavez and followed the stranger.

Although Elliot found all of this strange, it was now his turn to eat the incessant dust. No one envied the drag position, but somebody had to do it. He pulled his neckerchief up over this face, but already tasted grit in his mouth.

He glanced over to his right beyond the herd and noticed Rafer riding easy, his bum leg draped over the saddle horn. Rafer saw him and waved.

Elliot wondered as to why the white man ever decided to settle this barren wasteland. Better they should have left it with the Indians who were the only ones who appreciated it. And the Indians resented the white intrusion as well. The Indian couldn't be blamed for hating the white men, but the white renegades and Comancheros were something else again. Woe be unto a white woman that was unfortunate enough to become a captive to either of these groups. In the South, a woman was revered and pampered. But that was another world and years ago, Elliot mused.

That evening, they camped near a small, dirty creek which allowed the horses to drink their fill. Elliot felt filthy after riding drag all afternoon. He hoped that Chavez would place another drover in that unenviable position tomorrow.

Chavez, seemingly tireless, brewed coffee and cooked a meager supper. Night fell quickly when

Travis rode in, his horse spent and lathered. He dismounted, stretched, then slowly reached for a plate of beans. Chavez poured him some hot coffee.

"Damn, I'm tired," Travis said, stretching again. "It's been a long day."

"So, where you been all day?" Rafer asked.

Chavez interrupted. "Did you see the gringo that rode up this morning and talked to me? I did not know him and it bothered me that he kept looking at the horses. I did not trust him, so I asked Travis to follow him. If the stranger was a scout, I needed to know and we could change direction." He looked at Travis and continued, "and did you find out anything, amigo?"

"No, not really. He saw me and went into a run," Travis said, cupping his coffee in his hands and staring at the fire.

"Wonder why he went into a run?" Billy asked while stuffing his mouth with beans.

Travis looked at him, frowning. "I don't know why, except he probably meant to warn others and try to take the horses. Hell, I dunno. Why'd he spur his pony then?"

"Maybe he thought you were trying to do him in," Devon said.

"Well, whatever was the reason, tomorrow, amigos, we swing west, for a day at least," Chavez remarked.

"Hell, Chavez, that means we have to make up another day," Billy said.

"I know, my friend, but I cannot take the chance, and it could mean there may be shooting. I do not want that."

"Don't worry about it," Travis exclaimed.

They all turned and stared at him.

"What he means, Chavez, is that Travis here killed him," Billy said. "Ain't that right?"

Travis looked up at Billy with a crooked smile on his face.

"Madre mia," Chavez cried. "Is this true, Travis? Did you kill that man?"

Turning then to confront Chavez, Travis said, "Well, what did you want me to do? I did all of us a favor. He was probably going to warn others and maybe kill us and take the horses. Did you want that?"

"Did you back shoot him, Travis?" Billy said, smirking.

"Damn you, young'un, I tell you I had no choice. Now, let me be," Travis said, his mouth full.

Silence descended on the group for the remainder of the evening. Elliot tried to think of how Travis killed the man and if the man was, in truth, a waylayer. He really could have been innocent enough, but Elliot dreaded to think about that.

Chavez sat near the fire, his thoughts bothering him. Noticing his uneasiness, Elliot sat down next to him.

"Maybe that fella was a scout," he said.

"Maybe," Chavez responded, not taking his eyes off the fire, "but it is not good to take a man's life without knowing for certain. You understand?"

"Yes, I understand."

"I have seen too many people die in this country, amigo," Chavez lamented. "There are those that are jealous of my patron because of all his land. There are savages that wish to have their lands back and there are those that just move around with hate in their hearts. It never stops."

"One day, Chavez, I'm sure that it will stop after law and order gets ahold here."

"Perhaps, but it is sad that I may not be here to see it, my friend. But enough of this. It is time to sleep."

Elliot laid down and thought for a brief moment. Chavez was a caring individual. He liked that and liked working for him. His eyelids slowly closed.

Later, the wailing of a coyote awoke him. Looking around, he noticed Chavez was also awake. Their eyes met.

"Kind of odd, ain't it?" Elliot whispered.

'It is not the coyote, my friend," Chavez responded. Devon's intermittent snoring seemed to drown out the howling coyote.

"I'm afraid that we may have company by morning, amigo," Chavez said. "But, you sleep while I stand guard for awhile."

Rafer, momentarily awaking, heard the conversation.

The next morning was clear and cool, as breakfast was quickly consumed. Chavez recounted the horses. They were all there and he breathed a sigh of relief.

As they cinched their mounts, Rafer looked over the back of his horse toward Chavez. "I was hoping we could've gotten around any Injun trouble, boss."

"My friend," Chavez said, smiling, "the Indian has eyes everywhere. What they do not see, they hear. As we must travel by day and in the open, so they must look and hide. Now, we must watch the horses closely. I need someone to stay with the horses if we have trouble."

"I'll do it," Rafer said.

'Thank you, amigo." As Chavez mounted, he warned the others to be on the alert.

Elliot checked his navy colt and loaded his Winchester rifle. His rifle was far more efficient than the single shot breech loader he had used during the war. The Winchester was not as cumbersome nor as noisy, and the action much smoother. He felt comfortable with it, yet he was nervous. His heart was racing as he, too, swung up into the saddle and dug his boots deep into the stirrups. He rubbed Toter's neck. She might become pretty busy today.

The men took their positions and the drive resumed. The morning hours revealed no sign of any hostiles.

Elliot paced his mount to saddle up next to Chavez around noon. "It seems strange that they hadn't attacked by now, don't it?" he said.

"Yes, amigo, but there may not be many of them, and they know we are better armed. Yet one does not know how the Indian thinks. You expect one thing and they do something else. Rather I lose my right arm than lose any of my patron's horses."

"I understand," Elliot said, knowing full well Chavez meant every word he said.

"I have been with Senor Paolo all of my life," Chavez continued, "and he is a good and kind man. Any of the ranch hands would die for him."

Turning in the saddle, Elliot looked at the others, who had bunched the horses tightly.

"Wouldn't it be better if we spread the men out a little more?" he said.

Turning around, Chavez nodded. "You are right, Elliot, I was not thinking. Please, see that it is done. Oh, and see that your friend, Summers, comes forward and takes my place."

As they rode on, the thought came to Elliot that maybe they wouldn't be attacked after all. He noticed that Chavez was ranging back and forth, keeping an eye out for danger. As he strained to see Rafer up front, a glint caught his eye. It was coming from a low hill in front of them. If it was a glint, then that meant that the Indians out there had guns. He did not like the thought of facing a bunch of Indians with modern guns. Glancing at his companions, he raised his hand and pointed forward. It won't be long now, he mused.

The hair on the nape of his neck prickled, and he squeezed his knees against his horse. He turned and saw Billy, who smiled at him and doffed his bowler. Damn, Elliot thought, Billy is a cool one while he, himself, was scared to death. Even in the saddle, he had the urge to urinate. The feeling of anxiety was all too familiar, reminding him of the war and the charging Blue bellies. He unsheathed his Winchester lever action and held it at the ready.

Then he saw them - charging over the low rise. They emitted wild chilling screams as they came straight for them. The abrupt noise made Toter shy. He held his horse in check as he tried to count the savages. He saw only three. Surely a mere three Indians weren't stupid enough to take them on. Perhaps the beautiful horses they were herding though, spurred the savages to take chances. However, within a split second, he saw three more raise a dust cloud off to his left, heading straight for Devon. Still, only three of the Indians were toting guns, somewhat of a relief. The others brandished spears and war clubs.

Satisfied that there were only six in all, he drew down on the closest Indian while trying to steady Toter. But trying to pick his target through the dust cloud was not easy. Before he could pull the trigger, though, a shot rang out behind him, and the half naked savage toppled off his pony, rolling almost to his pony's hooves. Elliot turned around to see that Billy had drawn first blood. Then, he swung off Toter and knelt down. Fingering back the hammer, he settled the Buckhorn sight on another Indian. The gun roared, with the slug knocking the red headband off the top of his head. The Indian cart wheeled off his horse's back. Hell, Elliot thought, if the bullet didn't kill him that hard fall would. Briefly, he thought of the Murtaugh giant.

As Elliot was wondering how Rafer was faring in an attempt to stay with the stampeding horses, a yelling, painted Indian swooped down on him. Instinctively ducking, the Indian's war club missed his head by inches. Falling backward, Elliot shot as the Indian lunged at him. The slug caught the Indian in the thigh but did not deter him in the least. Not having the time to rechamber a cartridge in his rifle, he threw it down and drew his colt. The slug tore through the Indian and he somersaulted past.

Swirling dust made it difficult for him to distinguish between friend or foe as charging shadows raced through the haze. Cocking his pistol, he wiped his eyes hurriedly and saw a mounted form coming at him. He raised his colt only to notice at the last minute that it was Billy.

"Yahoo," Billy shouted, as he raced past Elliot.

Damn him, thought Elliot. He was enjoying this, while his whole body was shaking. Billy should have been at Antietam instead of him. He hated the war and the gore associated with it.

Elliot, kneeling, spun around, cocking his single-action again. Satisfied there were no more hostiles bearing down on him, he raised up. The battle had ended as quickly as it had begun. He raced to his horse, jumped on her back, and rode off in the direction of the frenzied horses. Where was Rafer? Maybe he's dead, killed by the Indians or fallen beneath the horses' thundering hooves.

Sweat was pouring down Elliot's face as he lashed at his mare's flanks in order to overtake the horses. He looked around to make sure no Indians were close and then noticed the horses ahead were slowing. At that moment, he saw Rafer pulling back on the lead stallion. Seeing Rafer in control calmed him, and he, too, slowed. Finally, the thoroughbreds were checked.

Weary, Elliot reined up, dismounted, and sat down, cursing. He wiped his face with his filthy bandana.

"You all right, Elliot?" Rafer asked, striding up to him.

"Hell yes," Elliot replied, "but I'm so damned bushed, I just want to lay here and catch my breath. Whew."

"Swamdoogle," Rafer shouted. "That was sure something, weren't it?"

"Partner, I don't need anymore of this," Elliot commented. "I just put on a few more gray hairs." "Better gray hair than no hair at all," Rafer said, laughing. "So, how many did you kill?" "I don't know and I don't care," Elliot said. Chavez rode over. "Are you all right, amigos?"

Both nodded.

"Senor Travis has been wounded and I must attend to him. Rafer, please count the horses and we will stay here for the night."

"Hey, Chavez, wait a minute," Rafer called. "Just what kind of Indians were they anyway?"

"Comanche, my friend. Now I must go."

Chavez and Rafer rode off in different directions.

Elliot was still trying to relax when Billy and Devon rode up.

"You all right?" Devon asked, dismounting.

Elliot nodded, still breathing heavily.

"Hey, Elliot, how did you like that first shot I made, huh?" Billy asked.

"It was a fine shot, Billy, and thanks," Elliot replied. "Did you do that with a hand gun?"

"Sure did "

"Then that was a hell of a shot from that distance, and mounted, too," Elliot said.

'Boy, them Indians can sure ride, can't they?" Devon said. "They was on us before we knowed it."

Elliot arose, dusting himself off, and then noticed that Devon's horse was bleeding. He mentioned it to Devon.

'Well, damn it anyway," Devon said, running his hand on his horse's chest. He dismounted, cursing. "Now what do I do? He ain't gonna last long with that hole in him."

"If I was you," Billy said, "I'd try to get me one of them Indian ponies but, like as not, you're gonna have to break him in again. They're used to that God awful Indian smell." He checked his gun and smiled.

Laughing, Devon said, "Shouldn't be no problem, cause I smell bad, too. It would be nice if Chavez let me ride one of them breeds we got."

"I wouldn't even chance asking him if I was you," Billy said.

"You're right. Well, do you mind lassoing one of them Indian broncs for me?"

"Okay," Billy replied, wheeling his horse. "Be back in a minute."

"Them Comanche was a bit north of their stomping grounds, weren't they?" Devon asked.

"Hell, I don't know. Seems to me them devils go where they please," Elliot said, rubbing his horse's flanks for wounds. Satisfied that his horse had no injuries, he retrieved his canteen and took a drink.

Rafer returned. "What's Billy doing out there?"

Devon explained that his horse had been injured and Billy was to bring him an Indian pony.

"Well, we lost two horses, fellas," Rafer commented. "Chavez ain't gonna like it, but..."

"Better them than us, eh?" Devon said.

Elliot, looking over the herd, once again spied the black stallion. He would give anything to own that one, but then chided himself for even thinking about it.

In a few minutes, Billy returned, leading a painted pinto, who appeared docile enough. In the meantime, Devon had removed his saddle and had casually thrown it on the ground.

"You may as well shoot him," Elliot said. "He's gonna die anyway."

"Yeah," Devon replied. "You're right, but it's a shame." He led the wounded animal away from the presumed campsite. In a few moments, a shot rang out, and then he solemnly returned as Chavez and Travis rode in. Travis had a nasty, bloody bandage wrapped around his upper arm. He got off slowly and sat down.

"How bad is it?" Billy asked, looking at Travis.

"Amigos, it is bad," Chavez said. "The spear went clear to the bone, and I fear he needs the attention of a doctor, and soon."

"Chavez," Rafer said, "we lost two of the horses."

"Well, it is lucky we did not lose more, my friend."

Elliot was surprised that he had taken it so well, but realized that at the moment, Chavez was thinking more of the wranglers. They had been lucky indeed.

Everyone was tired, and after a quick meal, relaxed before bedding down.

Chavez went to the pack mule and rummaging around, pulled out a bottle. Seeing it, Rafer's eyes widened.

"What you got there, boss?" he inquired.

"Tequila, my friend."

"Lord, let me have a snort of that," Rafer said, wringing his hands in glee.

The bottle was passed around and quickly consumed.

"You got another?" Devon asked, wiping his lips.

"I'm sorry, no, my friend," Chavez said sadly. "But it is just as well. Tomorrow we must be clear headed again."

Sleep was a blessing and Elliot heard Travis moaning at times. He felt sorry for the man.

Sometime before dawn, Chavez woke Elliot and asked to be relieved before daylight.

4

lliot lit a cigarette as he watched the sun peek over the horizon. Everything was so peaceful, he reveled at the stillness. The others began stirring when he rode back to the campsite.

Before long, they resumed their northward march. That afternoon, they stopped at a small stream, and after letting the tired horses drink their fill, they stripped and bathed in the turbid water. It was a very refreshing respite.

The following day, the weather was a bit cooler, and the riders, although again dirty, were a bit more comfortable.

In the evening, Chavez unwrapped the bandage from Travis' shoulder, and upon examining the wound closely, said, "I'm sorry, Travis, but your wound is not healing well. You must see a doctor pronto or you will lose your arm."

Looking at it, Elliot agreed with him. He had seen and smelled gangrene before, and this was the early stages of the dreaded malady.

"Well," Tom admitted, "it ain't got much feeling in it anyway."

"All I can do is try to put a clean bandage on it for now," Chavez said, "but that will not be enough." He turned to Elliot. "Senor, tomorrow, you will take him to the doctor in El Paso quickly. He must have his arm attended to. It is only a half day's ride for the two of you because we will only hold you up. You understand?"

"Yes, Chavez," Elliot countered, "but what do I do for money?"

"Do not worry, I will give you money, amigo."

As they were about to depart for El Paso the next morning, Chavez gave Elliot twenty dollars.

"Senor Travis, if you are unable to continue with us, I will understand and I will send back more money for your trouble," Chavez said. "Now, we will be passing El Paso in two nights and you can meet us five miles beyond near the banks of the Rio Grande. Go with God, the two of you."

"I'll be back, Chavez," Travis replied. "You can be looking for me."

The two left the group, moving at a good pace toward El Paso. Rafer watched as they departed. This was the first time he and Elliot had been separated in many years.

As they rode North, Elliot tried to get to know Travis better.

"Say, Tom, that Laredo is a good town. How come you left?"

"I had a good job there, Elliot, and a lot of good friends. I was married to a fine woman and had a little girl, too, but..."

"But what?" Elliot asked.

"But, I'd get drunk once in awhile and beat her." He turned and looked Elliot square in the eye. "I can't hold my liquor, man. I start drinking and sometimes I go crazy." He rubbed his sore arm and continued. "Well, finally my woman left me and took the child. Hell, I don't blame her at all."

"Did you ever try to find her again?"

"Yeah, but I couldn't find her. Maybe, I hope, she found a better life. I think about the two of them all the time and I curse that damn whiskey." "Your arm hurts bad, don't it?" "Yeah, it's throbbing something awful." "Well, it won't be long now and we'll get you fixed up good as new."

El Paso Del Rio Del Norte was a small, dirty, but thriving village of perhaps five hundred residents, most of whom were Mexican. It was the final gateway to the north and to New Mexico. A frontier town, it contained a few notable lawmen and a lot of infamous badmen. To the east was the Guadalupe mountain range, and to the immediate west was the shallow Rio Grande river. South and west of town was a federal army post habitated by calvary personnel called "Yellow Legs" because of the leggings they wore.

Elliot and Tom rode in unannounced in the early afternoon. Elliot stopped and asked a passerby where the doctor's office was located. Receiving directions, they continued until they were abreast of the "Last Chance" saloon. The name was quite common throughout the territory, Elliot mused.

"Hey, Elliot," Tom said, "let's have a drink before we see the doctor, huh?"

"Why not," Elliot replied. "But just one, because we need to get you to the doctor bad, partner."

Elliot felt that a solid whiskey might make the doctor's visit a little easier for the both of them.

Tom downed the shot of rotgut even before Elliot had lifted his and quickly ordered another.

The bartender poured it for him. Then, seeing the dirty bandage, he said, "Say, mister, I hope that you're going to see Doc Adams. That thing looks bad."

"Mind your own business, barkeep," Tom declared. "My partner and myself are gonna have another drink."

"No, we're not, Tom. That's enough for now. Maybe later, but we're going straight to the Doc's office," Elliot said.

Travis followed Elliot to the doctor's small office. They didn't have to wait long. The doctor removed the bandage from Tom's arm and then looked up. "It's good you came when you did, son. You could easily have lost that arm, or even your life. Now, let's clean it up first, get that dead skin off, and see what we've got."

'Tom, while he's working on you, I'll go get us a hotel room for the night," Elliot said, not wanting to watch the gore or listen to the pain. "I'm kind of bushed. When he gets done, you come on over. That all right?"

"Sure, partner, go ahead," Travis replied. "I'll be over there in a little while."

"Hold still, son," the doctor scolded as Tom fidgeted.

Elliot departed and made straight for the hotel. Entering the lobby, he went to the desk and a bespectacled elderly man turned the register book toward him. Then he wearily climbed up the stairs with his saddle bag and walked in the room. Although clean, it smelled of burnt mesquite, and he noticed the flowery wallpaper, which was not common to hotels he had visited before. No mind, he was tired, and without undressing, he pulled his boots off and collapsed on the small bed, quickly falling asleep.

Elliot bolted upright. What was that, he thought groggily. It had sounded like a gunshot, but it was so sudden, he wasn't sure exactly what it was. He sat up and wiped his face. Momentarily, he had forgotten where he was, then his mind cleared. Looking out he saw that it was getting dark. So where was Travis? He wondered how long he had been asleep. Then he got out of bed and walked over to the basin. Pouring a small amount of water in it, he doused his face. Cupping his hand, he dipped into the water and rinsed his dry, stinking mouth. With wet fingers, he slicked back his hair.

Surely, Tom still wouldn't be at the doctor's office this long unless there was a complication. Pulling on his boots, he left and went downstairs. Brewing coffee in the small dining room smelled too good to pass up, so he went in, sat down and obtained a cup. As he placed the cup to his lips, he overheard a couple of men whispering about a shooting at the saloon. Well, he thought, that had indeed been a gunshot that woke him up.

He quickly finished the store-bought coffee, then left. He noticed a few townsfolk milling around the saloon as he walked toward the doctor's office.

Inside, he noticed that Travis wasn't around, nor was the physician. At that moment, the doctor entered from another room, wiping his hands with a towel.

"Oh, Doc," Elliot said, "I was wondering about the man I brought in? You know, the man with the wounded arm. Is he still here or what?"

"Yeah, he's here, my boy," the doctor replied, "but I wasted my time working on him."

"Huh? I don't understand."

"He's dead, son," the doctor said.

"Dead? How can that be. From a bad arm?"

"Hell son, forget the arm. He's got a hole in his back as big as a hen's egg. So, where were you?"

"I was over at the hotel resting and Travis was to meet me there when you got finished with him," Elliot said, unbelieving.

"Travis, that's his name?" the doctor said. "He never told me. Anyway, he got killed over at the Last Chance. Yep, wasted my time working on that arm. Shame. I thought I done a pretty good job, too."

"What happened, anyway?" Elliot asked, stunned.

"Better you ask the sheriff about that. By the way, I'm the town mortician, too," the doctor said.

Elliot turned to leave.

"Hey, boy, what do you want me to do with the body?"

Elliot reached in his pocket and drew out some money. "Here, will this be enough?"

"I suppose it will have to do," the doctor answered. "I'm sorry about your friend."

Elliot left, heading straight for the sheriffs office, where he asked about the circumstances surrounding Tom's death.

"Well," the sheriff began, "seems like your friend went to the Last Chance and ordered a couple of drinks, then tried to take a young girl away from her boyfriend. Mind you, from what I hear, they were minding their own business. Anyway, your friend got a little nasty and told the young lad to skedaddle. The girl, trying to keep a fight from happening, got up from her table and was following your friend to another table. Then the young boy jumped up and pulled a pistol and shot your friend in the back. That's about it. Say your friend's name was Tom Travis, huh?"

"Yeah, sheriff, Tom Travis," Elliot said. "We was out on a drive to New Mexico."

"Who are you wrangling for?" the sheriff inquired.

"I'm with Chavez Ramon. We're taking some horses to Las Cruces."

"Hmm, Chavez is it?" the sheriff said. "He's a good man, with the Lazy P."

"Sheriff, what about the boy that killed Travis?" Elliot asked.

The sheriff pointed behind him. "He's locked up, why?"

"Can I see him?" Elliot asked, looking around.

"Sure, just leave your iron on the desk here."

Opening the door, he showed Elliot the cell where the young boy was held. He looked up at Elliot stoically as he approached the bars. Then Elliot shook his head and walked out.

"Sheriff, that boy ain't even old enough to shave yet," Elliot said, bewildered.

"Old enough to pull a trigger, son."

"So what's gonna happen to him?"

"He back shot a man. Probably get hung just like his pa before him. He comes from a mean family, and your friend picked on the wrong folks. Anything else?"

Elliot shook his head, holstered his pistol and started for the door.

"Tell Ramon hello for me," the sheriff said, turning back to his paperwork.

It was now dark as Elliot strode over to the Last Chance and ordered a drink. Looking down, he saw a large dried blood stain on the floor. Surveying the room, though, he did not see any young girl that would've been the catalyst for the shooting.

Finishing his drink, Elliot departed for the hotel. Why couldn't Tom had come straight back there like he was supposed to? Maybe I should have stayed with him, Elliot thought, and this wouldn't have happened. Damn it, why should I have to nursemaid the man? What am I gonna say to Chavez? He cursed.

He did not sleep well thinking that Chavez might blame him for not watching over Tom more closely.

The next day, Elliot started out late, knowing he would be ahead of the herd anyway. Stopping at a livery stable, he sold Travis' horse and saddle for thirty dollars.

He would have liked to forward this money to Tom's widow, but he would have a problem finding her. He remembered that Tom couldn't find her anyway.

The road leading north out of El Paso was lined with cottonwood trees, a soothing, pleasant sight. A slight breeze made the leaves shimmy, which reminded him of Dallas. He noticed many Indians and Mexicans camped along the Rio Grande banks, some of whom tried to hawk their food and cheap trinkets to him. At noon, he lingered long enough to purchase a tortilla and a sack of tobacco. Later, when civilization petered out, he stopped and made a cold camp. A passing Mexican, riding a burro, stopped long enough to share coffee with him and then continued on.

Laying back, Elliot suddenly wondered about what had brought him to this place at this time in his life. Had he and Mary Louise married, he most likely would have remained in Dallas, but what kind of work would he do? He could have worked for the railroad like his father, but he enjoyed the outdoors too much for that. Looking up, he reveled at the clear night sky, resplendent with huge, bright, blinking stars. A half-moon was sneaking up in the eastern horizon. No, he would not have been happy working for the railroad. All he knew is that he would have been a good husband and he wondered, had they got married, what would their children have looked like?

As he pondered, the thought came to him as how he was to break Tom's demise to Chavez.

Damn.

Early the next morning, he spotted the herd with Chavez still in the lead. Saddling up, he joined them.

"Good morning, amigo," Chavez said, looking around. "It looks like Travis decided to leave us after all."

"Oh, he left us all right," Elliot said, remorsefully. "He's dead."

"Dead, but the arm — he could have lost the arm, but not his life," Chavez said with a puzzled look on his face.

Elliot related the tragic incident to Chavez and later took his position on the flank of the herd. Rafer waved to him and grinned.

That evening, while they camped, Elliot told the other wranglers what had happened. Spooning some beans into his mouth, Billy looked up and said, "Was she a looker, Elliot?"

"The girl, you mean? Hell, I don't know. I never saw her," Elliot replied, trying to sew a tear in one of his shirts.

"Ain't no sense in dying over a gal that ain't a looker, now is it?" Billy said.

"Oh, shut up," Devon said, disgusted.

Billy laughed as chewed beans spit out of his mouth.

"It may be God's retribution for Travis killing that stranger before," Chavez said.

"Elliot," Rafer whispered, leaning over, "what's that word, retri..retri..?"

Elliot waved him off.

"Until we reach the ranchero, Elliot," Chavez continued, "you will be by yourself on the left flank. I just hope that we do not have any more troubles, amigos. I cannot face my patron if we lose any more men or horses."

After bedding down for the evening, Elliot lay awake, thinking about Travis and then the soft hotel bed and briefly about Mary Louise. His mind was racing therefore sleep was late in coming. A slight noise jerked him awake. He heard something akin to a scraping sound. It could've been one of the horses, but he fine tuned his hearing. His mare was shuffling nervously, and it wasn't like her to do this unless she was spooked.

Elliot turned on his belly and moved his eyes, staring into the darkness for any sign of danger. Toter stirred again, and this time, she snorted softly. Looking around, Elliot saw that everyone was sound asleep, all, that is, except Chavez. They looked at one another briefly. Elliot laid his finger across his lips and began crawling into the darkness. After a minute, he stopped, listened and resumed crawling. He tried to discern any foreign movement amid the shadows of the horses milling about, then he noticed a shadowy figure stooping low and moving silently toward the herd.

Rising to his knees, Elliot groped for a knife sheathed in his boot. Trying not to lose sight of the mysterious figure, he felt sweat bead up on his forehead. Slowly, he reached up to wipe his eyes while focusing on the figure, who was moving his way. Good, thought Elliot, better he move than me. A mesquite shrub was blending his outline from the intruder. Just come a little closer, Elliot thought, just a mite closer. Again his heart was racing. When the shadowy figure was just about upon him, Elliot lunged, catching the stranger above the knees and bowling him over. He knew it was an Indian immediately, as the smell of an unwashed body reached his flared nostrils. The Indian, agile, somersaulted into a standing position, then raised an object that looked like the dreaded war club. He was small, but most Indians in these parts were.

Elliot stood up, poised with his knife extended. He wished for his gun, but a shot at this time of night would stampede the animals. They were agitated enough as it was. Raising his club, the Indian leaped toward him. The club came around but Elliot deftly moved inside of the swing and felt his knife sink into the Indian's thigh. The savage screamed and fell backward. Elliot pulled back, startled. The scream sounded like that of a child.

His companions rushed forward, with Chavez holding a fire brand aloft. Elliot looked closely. It was a young Indian and his wide eyes revealed that he was very frightened.

"Well, I'll be damned," Rafer shouted, "he can't be more'n fourteen years old."

"Yeah, they start them to stealing pretty young, don't they?" Devon said.

Billy, holstering his gun, laughed. "Hell, Elliot, you ain't gonna notch this one up, are you? He don't weigh a hundred pounds soakin' wet."

Chavez approached the Indian and spoke in Spanish. The boy merely looked at him, but did not respond.

"Maybe he don't savvy Mex," Rafer remarked.

"Oh, he understands all right," Chavez said, then he repeated himself.

Looking around, the boy was obviously looking for a way to escape. He did not appear to be in pain as blood trickled down his leg. Elliot and the rest knew better, though, but the Indians were tough, taught to disregard any show of pain.

Chavez, still speaking in Spanish, waved his hand into the night. The Indian hesitated then fled, the night swallowing him.

"He desired one of our horses, amigos. If he returned to his wickiup with one of these, he would have instantly become a warrior in good stead. But, he will not bother us again. Come, let us get some sleep."

"Damn, I'm glad I didn't kill that boy," Elliot said to Rafer. "I just couldn't live with myself."

"Swam doogle, Elliot, he meant to kill you. Besides, it was dark. How was you to know."

"Yeah, but still..."

5

Late the next day, they crossed the Rio Grande and swung west of Las Cruces, New Mexico, riding north for a few miles. Then Chavez raised his hand and beckoned the riders to come forward.

When they had gathered around him, he said, "Amigos, you are now on senor Paolo's land, the Lazy P. As far as you can see is our range."

Elliot scanned the horizon and seeing mountains to his left, pointed and asked, "What's that range called?"

"The Black Mountains, amigo. The Mescalero Apache consider it sacred country, but it is many miles from here," Chavez said.

Elliot had to admire the heavy concentration of cottonwood trees and isolated patches of scrub pines. It was pretty country and he also noticed a sprinkling of cattle grazing in the distance.

"Come, amigos," Chavez declared, "we still have a long way to go before we reach the hacienda. We will camp for tonight at a line cabin so that you may sleep with a roof over your head."

"That would be a hell of a change," Billy said, gleefully. "My back is killing me."

At long last, a small log cabin came into view. On its east side was a corral, but it was not big enough to hold the numerous horses.

Elliot watched as the beautiful black stallion pranced among his charges.

It was a pleasure to sleep under a roof, even though there were not enough beds for everyone. Billy and Devon were allotted the two beds. Devon's snoring reverberated throughout the cabin all night, but the only one that remained awake from it was Rafer. It showed the next day as he was practically asleep in the saddle.

Early that afternoon, the group topped a rise and there below stood a magnificent, white washed adobe house with a red tiled slate roof. Cascades of crimson bougainvillea draped from the eaves, almost hiding the house. Stark white stone walks led to several entrances and surrounding the house, fenced corrals spread out like tentacles in all directions. Huge cottonwoods cast moving shadows across the structure as Elliot could only marvel at the sight. It was a palatial mansion in the middle of nowhere.

Refer glanced over at Elliot as he, too, was thoroughly impressed by the sight they beheld. "You ever in your life seen anything like that?" Refer said, taking off his hat and scratching his head.

"It is pretty, for a fact," Elliot replied.

Billy rode up beside them. "How about that, gents? I ain't seen nothing that elegant since I left New Orleans."

"Hell, this Paolo must be the richest man in these parts," Rafer commented.

Chavez rode up. "Amigos, we are not finished. We must get the horses in the corral."

They guided the thoroughbreds to the corral nearest the house, and then Chavez closed the gate on them. When he turned, Elliot noticed a big smile on Chavez's face, a sight up to now not seen by Elliot.

The sweet smell of flowers filled Elliot's nose, and he thought that the abundance of flowers was a woman's touch. He also thought of the fifty dollars due him.

Then he noticed a young woman standing near the hacienda, her hands on her hips. She sported a lithe figure and ebony hair which was half-hidden by a black, flat brimmed hat, with the chin strap tucked smartly under her chin. Her shapely legs were encapsulated in dark tight pants. A laced, thin, creamy blouse covered her upper body along with a dark red embroidered bolero. Black, ankle length boots completed her ensemble. She was the most beautiful creature Elliot had ever seen and he quickly surmised by her posture that she had to possess a mind of her own. Looking around quickly, Elliot noticed that all activity had ceased as everyone else was staring at her, too. He felt a blush coming on.

Rafer finally moved his horse closer to Elliot. "Will you look at that, Elliot," he whispered, cocking his hat further back on his head. It was a redundant statement because Elliot had been staring ever since he saw her.

Finally, the young woman felt that the newcomers had had enough of an eyeful and began walking towards them. It was obvious she was pleased by the attention as she smiled. As she approached, Billy rose in the saddle and took off his bowler. Seeing this respectful gesture, she nodded slightly.

Chavez took off his sombrero and advanced to meet the young woman. They spoke quietly and briefly and then he turned, escorting her to the corral. She stole a glance Elliot's way and smiled again. He felt his knees shaking. After a brief look at the horses, she and Chavez turned to them.

"Muchachos, may I introduce to you my patron's daughter," Chavez said, beaming. "This is Senorita Maria Evita Paolo."

The riders dismounted as she walked up to each and shook their hand. Elliot's head was swimming as the scent of jasmine perfume drifted toward him. He studied her face closely. She had dark eyebrows and long eyelashes. Her lips were full and outlined with ruby red lipstick. She couldn't have been more than twenty years old.

Completing the greetings, she stepped back and said, "Gentlemen, on behalf of my father and myself, I thank you for bringing these horses here safely. They are beautiful, are they not?"

Each wrangler voiced his agreement.

"Tonight, each of you will be my guest for dinner. I hope that you compliment us with a healthy appetite. We dine promptly at eight." Then she turned and briskly retreated to the hacienda.

Elliot mused that she did not mince words, coming straight to the point. He had never met such a woman.

Billy fanned himself with his bowler. "Boys, I've seen a lot of beauties back in old New Orleans, but this filly will beat them all."

"And she's got class, too," Rafer remarked.

As the senorita reached the stoa of the house, she stopped momentarily, glanced back and continued.

"Lord, what is a thing like that doing stuck way out here?" Rafer whispered.

They all turned as Chavez addressed them.

"Amigos, you have been honored this evening. Never have any ranch hands been invited to eat in her presence. I must ask that you address her with respect at all times. As you know, she is young and attractive, but remember, she is the only daughter of my patron, and any disrespect toward her will dishonor me. I hope you all understand me." He paused to look fixedly at each one of them. "After you have made yourselves presentable, I will escort you to the hacienda at eight o'clock this evening."

"Sounds pretty good to me, boys," Billy said, rubbing his hands.

Chavez beckoned to one of the Mexican ranch hands, who hurriedly came forward.

"This is Jose Estavez," Chavez said. "He will show you the bunkhouse and assign beds for you. He will also show you where you may clean yourselves. I must report to the senorita, but again, I thank you for your help and my patron will be grateful when he returns." He turned and made straight for the house.

As the group sauntered toward the bunkhouse, Elliot asked Jose if he had been here long.

"Si, senor, I have been here all my life as my father before me. Most of the vaqueros you see were born here as well."

"How many work here anyway?" Elliot asked.

"We have eighteen that work the ranch and there are two cooks and the house maid, Consuelo," Jose replied. "But we are still shorthanded."

"Hey, Jose," Billy said, "is the senorita married?"

"No, senor, she is not, but she is betrothed to a noble gentleman in Old Mexico, I think."

"Oh, so that's the way it is, huh," Billy said, trying to keep pace.

Arriving at the bunkhouse, Jose led the way in. The dirt floor was common enough, and the bunks, although neat, were small. Jose mentioned they could bathe in the cow pond to the rear and asked that each of them should shave as the Paolo family insisted on everyone being presentable when entering the main house. Then he left.

"How about this place, Elliot? Ain't it the most beautiful ranch you ever saw?" Rafer exclaimed.

"Yes it is, partner."

"I sure wouldn't mind staying here, to work I mean. This Mr. Paolo has got to have plenty of money," Rafer said, looking around.

"Well, there ain't nothing to keep us going, if we can get a job here, Rafe."

"I kind of like it, too," Billy said, "plus the senorita makes it more'n worthwhile."

"Let's walk around and look at this place, gents," Elliot said. "It sure is spread out."

Elliot and the others bathed, shaved, and put on relatively clean clothes. Elliot discarded his stinking long Johns for the time being.

Chavez came for them promptly at eight. Upon entering the house, Elliot was impressed by the elegant surroundings. The floor was made of smooth wood planking. Huge tapestries hung from the slatted walls, with mirrors and Spanish noblemen portraits interspersed. Strategically placed throughout was ornate furniture hewed from dark wood. Entering the dining room, they saw a large table capable of seating fifteen guests. On top of the starched white table cloth were neatly arranged spoons, forks, and knives, all made of gold. Devon's eyes bulged at the utensils.

A uniformed maid brought in a flask of dark red wine and placed it at the head of the table.

"My friends, this is Consuelo, who will serve you," Chavez said.

Consuelo glanced at them, bowed, and as she turned for the kitchen, the mistress of the house entered. Maria wore an off-shouldered, creamy white dress hemmed with lace, which complemented her white skin. A single red rose graced her ebony tresses.

Elliot's mouth went dry at the sight of her.

"Good evening, gentlemen," Maria said, "Please to sit. It is good of you to come. Consuelo, be so kind as to pour the wine for our guests."

Consuelo took the flask and filled their glasses after they had sat.

"Senorita," Billy said, "your home is beautiful."

"Thank you, senor. Senor Billy is it?"

"Yes, ma'am." He smiled, his face flushed.

Rafer said, "Your whole ranch is beautiful, ma'am."

"Again, thank you. Now," she said, "I would like to propose a toast for your successful trip bringing the prized horses to our ranch." She raised her glass, followed by the others.

"Do you find the wine to your taste," she said, looking at Elliot.

"Yes, ma'am, it's wonderful. I've never tasted such a wine. Just what is it?"

"I believe it must be a Madeira," Billy interrupted. "Am I right, senorita?"

"But, of course, Senor Billy," Maria said, "You are right. You know much of wines?"

"Well, being from New Orleans sort of gives me an edge on different wines, ma'am," Billy responded.

"I have heard much of this New Orleans. Perhaps one day I can visit such a wondrous city," Maria said. "You must tell me more of this place, later, perhaps?"

"Anytime, ma'am, anytime."

The aura of jasmine seemed to linger over the table, which made Elliot's mind wander to Mary Louise. Noticing his deep look, Maria said, "Excuse me, senor, is there something wrong?"

Coming back to his senses, Elliot replied, "No, nothing's wrong, senorita. My mind was wandering a little, that's all."

"Chavez told me that one of your companions died during the drive," she said, looking at each of them, "but he did not inform me of the circumstances of his death." Then she looked directly at Chavez.

"Senorita," Chavez responded, "the man Travis did not die because of the drive, rather..." he hesitated.

"Ma'am, he tried to steal another man's woman and was back shot in a saloon," Billy interrupted.

"Oh," Maria said, "I see."

She was much prettier than Mary Louise, Elliot mused, trying not to stare at her, and a hell of a lot younger.

"Senor Elliot," she said, changing the subject, "where is it you are from?"

"Dallas, ma'am," he replied.

"Me, too, ma'am. I'm from Dallas, too," Rafer interjected.

"Yes, Dallas, I was there a few years ago," Maria said, "It is nice. Do you have family there?"

"Well, I did, once, but they're all gone now," Elliot replied.

"You were in the war between the states, weren't you?" she inquired.

"Yes, m'am, but how did you guess?"

"I could tell by the way you act, senor. Forgive me, I do not mean to pry." She then turned to Devon,

"Are you from Texas as well, senor?" She was attempting to keep the conversation moving so her guests would be comfortable.

"Not exactly", Devon replied. "Oh, I was born in Texas, but my family left for California years ago. Someday, I hope to join up with them again or leastwise, I hope so."

A Mexican cook and an Indian maid began bringing in the food. There was a large platter of frijitos, followed by huge ears of white corn, sweet potatoes, and a vat of aromatic mutton, Elliot looked around and saw that the eyes of the other wranglers were bulging.

"Please, gentlemen, help yourselves," Maria said.

No further prompting was necessary, and the men began gorging themselves. Maria, taken aback by this display, merely lowered her eyes and smiled.

Elliot ate slowly, however, as his shrunken belly could not readily tolerate such rich food. Looking at Rafer, Elliot punched him, whispering that he needed to wipe his greasy chin.

"Pardon me, senorita," Devon asked, "but just what kind of meat is this anyway?"

"It is mutton, senor. Do you not like it?"

"Oh, yes ma'am. I just ain't never ate it like this before," Devon said.

"This wine, senorita," Billy said, swishing the liquid in his mouth, "where does it come from?"

"We buy the grapes from California, but we make the wine here, senor."

She lifted her glass again and drank, and Elliot thought that every move and gesture she made was a personification of grand upbringing.

"It certainly is a fine product," Billy responded.

Rafer wiped his mouth and burped. Embarrassed, he sheepishly looked in her direction. "I'm sorry, ma'am, but it couldn't be helped," he said.

"Please, don't apologize, Senor Rafer. It is a sign that you enjoyed your meal," she said, dabbing at the corners of her mouth with a napkin.

At the conclusion of the dinner, Consuelo returned, placing two bowls of hard, sweet candy on the table.

Devon leaned back in his chair. "I ain't never ate so good in my whole life," he said.

"Me neither," Rafer remarked, sucking on some candy.

"Thank you, gentlemen. I'm more than pleased," she said.

Elliot looked directly into her dark eyes. "I'm curious. What with all the Indians, the no-good whites, and the weather around these parts, it must be really hard to keep it going, the ranch I mean," Elliot remarked.

"Yes, senor, it is hard, as you say. My mother passed away five years ago, my two uncles were killed by Apaches and my only brother, God rest his soul, was slain by marauding Comancheros. We have lost several vaqueros to Indians and rustlers, but we persist to survive because this land is all we have."

Maria turned to Chavez, seated on her right, and whispered in his ear. He nodded, rose and left the room.

Maria took a deep breath and continued. 'There are many that wish us to give up this land, especially a few gringos that hate the Mexican. I remind you that the Spanish followed the Indian and settled this land years before the Americans. We try to live in peace with the Indians and the Americans, although at times, it is very frustrating."

"I understand, senorita," Elliot said sincerely.

In a moment, Chavez returned with a small sack. He sat down and poured out the contents. Gold coins clattered across the table as he quickly reached to pull them back.

"Senors, my father promised you this money for delivering the horses," Maria said.

Chavez counted each man fifty dollars in gold and handed it to them.

Maria continued. "My father had also asked Chavez to offer each of you a job if you wish to stay. You are welcome to work with us as Chavez trusts you. That, gentlemen, is a compliment few people will get from him." She smiled, looking up at Chavez, who paid her no mind.

"Senorita, thanks for the offer," Devon said, gathering his pay, "But I think I'll mosey on. I might want to go to the north country and maybe do some trapping. I just might get a notion to go on to California."

"If that is your desire, Senor Mitchell," she said. "Chavez, would you please to offer our guests cigars?"

Chavez brought a small wooden box and offered each man a cigar.

As they lit up the cigars one-by-one, Maria rose. She did not like heavy cigar smoke. Everyone rose in unison.

"Gentlemen, please be seated and enjoy your cigars. I must excuse myself, as it is getting late. Good night."

They said good night as she disappeared.

Walking back toward the bunkhouse, they discussed taking up Maria's offer.

"Well, fellas, what are you two going to do?" Billy inquired.

"As far as I'm concerned," Rafer remarked, "I'd just as soon stay right here. Hell, boys, I ain't never ate this good and besides, we been trying to find a place to settle. Ain't that right, Elliot?"

"I reckon so, partner," Elliot said. "I can't complain about this place at all."

"I guess I'll stay, too," Billy retorted. "Besides, it don't hurt my eyes to look at that Maria neither."

Entering the bunkhouse, they groped their way to their bunks, welcoming a permanent roof over their heads.

6

The next morning, they all arose before daylight. After rinsing his mouth and face, Elliot started toward the kitchen before Rafer had put on his clothes. Entering, Chavez met him and introduced him around. There were eight ranch hands at the table, not including Jose, who walked in at that moment.

"Amigo," he cried, "it is good to see you this fine day. Do you intend to stay with us?"

"Yep, I reckon so," Elliot responded, crossing the bench and sitting to eat.

"Good, I was hoping that, amigo," Chavez said, sitting down. "Then your friend, Rafer, will stay as well?"

Elliot nodded, reaching for flapjacks and syrup. The cook poured him some coffee.

A few minutes later, Rafer and Billy entered, joining the others. Devon had slept in as he was planning to leave anyway.

As the sun was rising, Chavez discussed their duties in and around the ranch. He finished by saying they were each to receive twelve dollars a month, as well as free room and board.

Gathering outside, they watched as Devon saddled his horse, mounted, then rode over to where they were.

"So, Devon, you been a good friend," Rafer said. " I wish you luck, partner."

"Thanks, and all you boys take care. Hope to see you again one day," Devon said, turning his pony

They watched as he headed north. Then Elliot glanced beyond Devon and saw a rider approaching. Elliot noticed that the rider looked Indian, but was dressed like a white man.

Chavez greeted the rider, then turned. "Amigos, this is Harry Two-Horse. He is our scout as well as the finest bronc-buster in the territory. Come, Harry, get down. Have you had breakfast?"

"No, Ramon," Harry said, dismounting. He shook hands with the new wranglers, and stopping in front of Billy, looked him up and down, with noticeable interest in the low hanging holster.

"You good with the pistola, mister?" Harry asked.

"I like to think so," Billy responded, grinning.

"He is modest, Harry," Chavez exclaimed. "He is very good." Then speaking to the others, he said, "Harry has been away checking the fences. He is, like you say, our trouble shooter."

Elliot looked toward the main house and saw Maria staring in their direction.

"Harry, you eat now and the rest of us will ride," Chavez continued. "I need to show them around the ranch."

As he turned, Harry looked up at the thoroughbreds milling in the corral. Glancing at Chavez, then Elliot, he said, "They are so magnificent, it surprises me that you did not lose them all to the Comanche. You are to be proud that you stayed alive to bring them."

"We were kind of lucky, Harry," Billy said, grinning broadly.

"Jose, bring the pack mule," Chavez shouted. "We go now."

On horseback, Chavez led the way followed by Elliot, Rafer, Billy, and Jose. Fat, sleek longhorn cattle were seen grazing as Chavez, at various times, pointed out landmarks. He wanted the newcomers to become familiar with the area. Several times they rode through bands of sheep, which scattered when they neared.

Elliot was in awe at the size of the spread and frequently let Chavez know about it.

They camped out that night and continued with the tour the following day.

"There to the north," Chavez pointed, "is Silver City, and to our east is the Rio Grande. Over there to the west are the Mimbre Mountains. At the foot of those mountains is a small, friendly Apache reservation. In the late fall before the snows come, my friends, you will be divided and sent to the line cabins that we have passed. There you will spend the winter taking care of the cattle within your district. Is that understood?"

"You got rustlers around here?" Billy asked.

"Yes, amigo, not many, but enough. Even one is too many, but should you find an Indian butchering a cow, he is to be left alone. He will not take more than he needs and they must live, too. This land, especially in the winter, is harsh. Here, let us stop and let the horses rest." Chavez and the others pulled up. It was now noon.

Jose retrieved some jerky and coffee from the satchel on the pack mule. In just a few minutes, the resting travelers were eating and drinking coffee.

Rafer stood up and looked far into the distance. "Just in case we do run into rustlers, Chavez," he said, "What do we do?"

Elliot thought it was a good question.

"You must use your mind, amigo. If there are many, just watch and report. If it is one, maybe two, you may capture them and we will turn them over to the sheriff in Las Cruces. Don't take unnecessary chances. The cattle are not worth one of us."

"How do you intend to split us up to stay in the line cabins?" Billy asked, wiping his mouth.

"In due time, amigo, I will select who is to go to which shack. I may want you, however, to stay at the ranch, Billy," Chavez said, casting his coffee aside.

"Why me, Chavez?" Billy inquired.

"The hacienda, my friend, is the hub of this entire ranch, and you are good with the pistol. Need I continue?"

Billy grinned and shook his head. "Hell, that's fine with me. I get to eat good grub, stay warm, and look at that fine filly of a senorita."

"Hear me, Billy," Chavez said sternly. "She is to be avoided. She is to marry another one day and any moves on your part will cost you your job. On this I must insist."

"Okay, okay, relax," Billy mumbled, as Chavez stared at him fixedly for a moment, then his face softened.

"Tomorrow, we will return to the ranch, but I want all of you to take a day soon and go to Las Cruces. I want you to meet the sheriff so that he will know that you work at the Lazy P. So, mount up, amigos."

They stopped at one of the line cabins just before dark. It was clapboard sided and contained one room with one window. There were two hardbacked chairs, a small table, a fireplace and two small cots. The dust was heavy in the cabin, but could easily be cleaned. Elliot had stayed in worse places. He just hoped that the roof didn't leak.

The next day, they started back toward the ranch.

Something was nagging at Elliot during the return journey. Looking over at Chavez, he said, "Tell me, just what is Senor Paolo's use for those thoroughbreds we brought in?"

Chavez grinned. "I was wondering when that question was to be asked. If we can crossbreed the Arabians to our quarter horses, we can introduce new bloodlines. The quarter horse is intelligent, but the Arabian has stamina. The quarter horse is bigger, but the Arabian is sleeker and takes the heat better. After a few years, our ranch will be able to sell better horses to the yellow legs at Fort Bliss. The calvary cannot afford to let these new breeds get away from them, so the price will be much higher, or so we hope."

"But there is a chance a new breed may not produce as you think they might," Elliot retorted.

"There is truth in what you say, amigo. This venture may be disastrous but my patron is willing to take that chance."

It was late when they returned to the ranch. Rafer was sorry that he had missed supper.

The next morning, after a hearty meal of beans, beef, and eggs, Elliot strolled around to familiarize himself with the area. There were several stables he had yet to see. He couldn't help but notice how clean the ranch area was kept. He met the blacksmith, who was the biggest Mexican he had ever seen, yet one of the most congenial. As they talked, he did not notice Maria, who came up behind him, but the blacksmith, looking beyond Elliot, saw her and removed his hat. Turning, Elliot also removed his.

"Good morning, Elliot," she said. "May I call you Elliot, senor?"

"Certainly, ma'am," he replied, uneasy in her presence.

"Come and walk with me. It will be a beautiful day."

As they walked slowly, Maria pointed out the ranch's features. He could tell that she was proud of her father's possessions, and from what he had seen, had a right to be.

They talked of the new horses and the ranch's attributes. Thankfully the Civil War was not brought up, as it was a sore subject for Elliot, but soon found that he, with Maria, could not avoid discussing his private matters altogether.

"Why is it that a handsome man such as you is not married?" she asked forthright.

Stunned, Elliot stopped for a moment and looked at her. Damn, he thought, she don't fool around with words.

"Just never got around to it, I suppose," he said, gathering his senses. "But I heard that you are to be married pretty soon, right?"

Then she stopped and he discerned a hurt look on her face.

"It was not of my choosing, I assure you," she said. "It was an arrangement my family had made when I was a little child. I have not seen him since I was nine years old."

"Who is him?" Elliot inquired.

"His name is Miguel Aragon. He comes from a wealthy family in Mexico City. It was my parent's wish that our two families join, but it makes me feel that I am a cow — to be traded in order to produce better stock," she said stoically.

This illustrative comment forced a smile from him, and she was quick to see it.

"Elliot, it is not a joke," Maria scolded.

"I'm sorry," he said straightening his face. "So, what do you intend to do about it?"

"I do not know. I don't wish to offend my father, but..."

At that moment, Elliot heard his name called. Turning, he saw Rafer running up.

"Hey, Elliot, are you going to town with me and Billy, or not?" Rafer shouted.

"Oh, I almost forgot about that," he said. "Senorita, will you excuse me? Chavez wanted us to meet the sheriff in Las Cruces."

She smiled. "Certainly, Elliot, but mind you, watch the women in that sinful town." The three wranglers mounted and as Elliot turned Toter, he glanced back at Maria. There she was again, hands on hips, with that defiant but still, beautiful look.

The village of Las Cruces was small, dusty, with a lot more Mexicans and Indians than Americans.

The three cowboys hitched their steeds to a rail in front of Mason's Bar and went inside. Elliot saw that there was a roulette wheel, several poker tables, a billiard table, and a long bar that stretched the entire length of the establishment. It was early in the day, so there were few patrons about. Seated behind the bar was an attractive, middle-aged lady and standing beside her was an unsmiling barkeep with a stubbled beard.

"Come in, gentlemen," the lady shouted. "Come in and have a drink. First one's on the house for strangers."

Billy and Rafer looked at each other, grinned, and strode up to the bar with Elliot following. The barkeep poured each a shot of whiskey, then they retreated to a table.

"Hell, this place is dead," Rafer said, looking around. "Ain't nothing happening."

Approaching them, the lady said, "it's too early, boys. Things don't get started around here until sundown."

Elliot couldn't help but notice the buxom figure this woman possessed. Although not beautiful, she was nonetheless attractive. Her long, red hair cascaded down and around her shoulders.

"Like what you see, cowboy?" she said, hands on her hips.

Elliot blushed. "I'm sorry, ma'am, if I was staring."

"You come with the drink, lady?" Billy asked, winking at her.

"No, cowboy, relax," she said. "My husband and me own this place. My name's Jenny Mason. My husband Sonny's in the back office. So where you fellas from?" she asked, resting her hand on Elliot's shoulder,

"We been hired by the Lazy P spread," Billy said, "but we come up from Texas, why?"

"The Lazy P, huh," she said. "Big outfit." She came around to look Elliot in the face. "And what's your name, handsome?"

Flustered, he replied, "Elliot Stewart, ma'am."

The office door opened and a pasty faced man emerged. He had slicked down blonde hair and sported a pencil-thin mustache. A red string tie hung between his tartan vest. As he came nearer, the strong aroma of cheap toilet water reached Elliot's nose.

"Jenny," the man said, "I'm on my way to El Paso. I'll be gone for a couple of days. Hello, boys."

The men nodded as he headed for the door.

"Sonny, if you find a nice dress at the Emporium, bring it home," she shouted. He waved without looking back.

"That, gentlemen, was my husband," Jenny said. "Fancy, ain't he?"

Billy laughed. "Miz Jenny, tell me, what's there to do in this cowtown?"

"Not much, cowboy, but if you want to gamble, this is the best place in town. We run an honest game - roulette, poker, Jack's Wild, you name it. Now, if it's a whore you want, you can find one at the north end of town. Just look for a two-story house with a white fence and red border flowers," she said, looking straight at Elliot. He blushed and looked away.

"How much for one of them whores?" Rafer asked.

"Oh, they get two dollars, maybe three," Jenny said. "A real looker might cost you four, but don't pay more than four, friend. You might start something other gents around can't stomach. Why, you interested, cowboy?"

"I sure am," Rafer said, grinning. "I ain't had me a woman in months, but I ain't had no money neither."

Jenny looked at Elliot. "How about you, big fella? You going to get you a whore, too?"

"No ma'am, not right now, anyway."

"Well, Mr. Elliot Stewart, perhaps you favor gambling," Jenny said.

"Yeah, I do, but right now, I'm going to have another drink, then walk around town and maybe get me a hotel room for the night," Elliot said.

"Our poker tables will be full come seven o'clock," Jenny replied. "Why don't you stop in and try your luck."

"I might just do that," Elliot agreed, lighting a cigarette.

"Well, Rafer, drink up," Billy said, grinning and finishing his whiskey, "and then let's you and me find that there whorehouse."

"I'm all for that," Rafer exclaimed. He rose along with Billy and bid Elliot good bye.

"He's a feisty young'un, ain't he?" Jenny said, watching the men disappear out the door.

"Who?" Elliot replied.

"That Billy there."

"Oh yeah, but he's okay, ma'am."

"Call me Jenny, will you? You make me sound old. You ain't married, are you?"

"No, ma'am, I mean Jenny, I ain't."

"How come?" she whispered. "A big good looking man like you."

Shifting nervously in his seat and wiping his brow, Elliot remarked, "Ain't seen no cause to get married, at least not yet anyway."

"Your friend, with the limp...."

"You mean Rafe?"

"Yes, Rafe. You two been together long?"

"Yep, we were in the war together," he said.

"That where he got the limp?"

"Yeah. He's the closest friend I got. We were mustered out together in Dallas."

She sat down and placed her hand on his leg. He stiffened, trying to move his leg.

"Relax," she whispered, "I ain't gonna bite you, hon. Here, have another drink." She poured his glass full. "This whole bottle ain't gonna cost you nothing."

At that moment, a fight broke out at one of the poker tables. Elliot jumped up, but Jenny calmed him. "Pay no mind, Elliot. Them yahoos do that all the time. They are friends, but you'd never know it. Sit down." Turning, she shouted, "You guys don't forget to pay for the damages before you leave."

Standing, Elliot said that he was going for a walk. Jenny shrugged, got up, and retreated toward the back office.

Seeing a small store, Elliot entered and purchased a new pair of denims, a cotton flannel shirt and a wool-lined heavy jacket. He also bought two pairs of long Johns. Packages in hand, he walked out only to come face-to-face with a friend.

"Devon," he said, "Well, I'll be damned. I thought you'd be in Montana by this time."

"Hello, Elliot. No, I wasn't in no hurry. Wanted to stay here for awhile, but I'll be leaving soon. Soon's my money runs out."

Elliot laughed.

"What are you doing in town?" Devon inquired.

"Oh, me, Billy, and Rafer came in for a couple of days. Chavez wanted us to get to know the sheriff, and I'd better do that, maybe tomorrow," Elliot reminded himself.

"Suppose I buy you a drink over at Mason's," Devon said.

"No, I just left there and I don't need another right now, but thanks," Elliot remarked.

"You met Jenny, ain't you?" Devon said, looking over at the saloon. "She's something else, boy, wouldn't you say?"

"Kind of pushy, Devon," he replied.

"Yeah, well, if you won't have a drink with me, then I'll mosey on. See you later."

Elliot watched as Devon continued past him.

Shaking his head, he resumed his walk. He saw the sheriff's office and also passed the house where his companions were. He entered the hotel, went to his room and only stayed long enough to drop his packages, clean up and put on new clothes. The sun was going down as he reentered Mason's Bar. Stepping up to the bar, he ordered a drink, just as Jenny reappeared.

"Well, Elliot," she said, looking him up and down, "you clean up real nice."

He nodded while looking past her.

"You gonna try your hand at poker?"

"I thought I might, for awhile, anyway."

"Just a word of warning, handsome," she said. 'Those guys there are good, so watch your money."

Taking his drink, he slowly made his way to the nearest table, where four hard cases were dealing.

"Mind if I join in, gents," he said. One man, not looking up, moved his chair over to make room for him.

Jenny followed him and tossed a new deck of cards on the table.

"Fellas, this here's Elliot Stewart. Now he's a friend, so treat him nice."

Sitting down, Elliot was informed of the stakes and raise limits. Several hands later, Billy and Rafer walked in.

"Well, I'll be damned," Rafer cried. "He's downright pretty, ain't he, Billy, all slicked up in them new duds."

"He's saving himself for me," Jenny said, laughing. Billy and Rafer laughed, too. Elliot tensed up at this remark.

Seeing his discomfort, Jenny remarked, "I'm just kidding, Elliot. Can't you take a joke?"

"Are we gonna play poker or talk all day," one of the players said disgustingly.

"Sorry," Elliot said. "Deal."

Elliot found his luck hard to believe. He had started with ten dollars and in no time it had grown to thirty-five. Billy and Rafer had retreated to a table and were getting drunk. It was late, and although tired, Elliot was on a winning streak and not about to quit. He ordered a full bottle of whiskey for the players at his table.

Two women walked in sometime later, and Billy, looking up, instantly recognized them. "Hey girls, over here," he yelled.

Both women, giggling, walked over and joined them. Elliot merely glanced their way.

"Barkeep," Billy shouted, "another bottle and fresh glasses here for the ladies."

"Ladies, ha," Jenny muttered to herself.

More customers arrived and the saloon was filled and becoming quite noisy.

A large man sauntered in about that time, and although drunk, Rafer stared at him. The man walked to the bar and ordered a drink, then turned to observe the action. Wiping his eyes, Rafer's mouth dropped.

"What's the matter?" Billy said, looking at Rafer. "You look like you seen a ghost."

"Huh? Oh no," Rafer said. The man looked familiar to him, but his mind was foggy at the moment. He took another drink of whiskey.

"Damn, Elliot," Jenny said, "you're having a hell of a win streak, ain't you?"

"Too much of a streak, if you ask me," one of the disgruntled players remarked.

"Look, Jim," Jenny said, "if you can't take the loss, then get out."

"Boys, I'm sorry," Elliot commented. "Maybe I just ought to quit."

"Quit? Hell no, man," another player said. "I want a chance to get some of my money back."

Elliot looked around the table, sensing that the other players felt the same way.

"All right, gents," he said, "I'll play two more hands, then win, lose, or draw, I'm leaving. I'm tired and a little drunk." It was his deal and he opted to play five card draw. He kept a pair of fives and drew three cards. Finally, opening his hand, he couldn't believe what he saw. He did not raise, although others did, while he merely called each raise.

"I got a diamond flush," Jim yelled. "Beat that, damn you."

Elliot looked at the diamond spread and revealed a full house, three threes and two fives. Staring at the winning hand, Jim banged his fist on the table, then rose to his feet.

He reached for a pistol nestled in his belt, but before he could draw, Elliot's gun barrel crashed down on this head. Jim pitched forward, scattering money in all directions.

Elliot, cocked his gun in front of the others. "Boys, now I played fair and square, and I don't want no more trouble. I'm gonna take ten dollars of that money and you can divvy up the rest."

Billy ran over. "Don't be no fool, Elliot, it's your money. Take it all."

"No, Billy, I said my piece," Elliot said, gathering up the money and thrusting it in his pocket.

Billy looked at the unconscious man. "Why didn't you gut shoot him? I would have."

"Let it go, Billy," Elliot said. "It's time I left."

As he turned, the others pulled Jim off the table and pounced on the remaining bills. Rafer walked over to him and tugged at his sleeve.

"What is it?" Elliot said, irritably.

"Elliot," Rafer whispered, "look at that hombre at the bar. Don't we know him?"

Elliot turned and saw the big stranger.

"Let's get out of here," Elliot murmured, and together, they quickly left. Outside, he stopped. "That must be that brother we heard about. You remember that Murtaugh man I shot before we got to Fort Stockton?"

"Huh? Yeah, yeah," Rafer cried. "That's who that is. They must've been twins. I knew I had seen him before."

"I never should have come to town, dammit," Elliot remarked. "Look at the trouble I've caused."

"Hell, Elliot, it ain't your fault," Billy said. "You should've kept your winnings, man. You're too easy."

7

Elliot was fast asleep when he felt his blanket being pulled. Although groggy, he rolled over abruptly and noticed a dark form moving beside him.

"What the....?"

"Shhh, Elliot, be quiet. It's me, Jenny."

"Jenny, what the hell are you doing in my bed?" he shouted, raising up.

"What do you think I'm doing, cowboy?" she retorted, pulling the covers up around her. Her naked body touched his and he leaped out of bed.

"Jenny, dammit, get out of my bed and put your clothes back on. You're a married woman."

Yeah, but Sonny's gone and I'm lonesome. Come on, Elliot, get back in bed. You won't be sorry, I promise you," she said, exposing her breasts.

He stared at her for a moment, his mind racing. "No, please, Jenny, this ain't right. I want you to leave."

"Listen, hon, Sonny's no good in bed. We ain't been together in months, and I got pressures. You know what I mean, now..."

"I can't help you, Jenny," he stammered. "Now, do as I say. Get your clothes on."

Tartly, she got up. "What's the matter, I'm not good enough for you? Why are you so high and mighty? You like men or something?"

"I just want to get a little sleep," he said. "Now, get out of here."

Dressing, she continued to swear at him. Then she pulled a small derringer out, but before she could cock it, he lunged and pried it out of her hand. He calmly walked over and tossed it out the window. As he turned back to her, she swung at him, but he spun her around, picked her up, and opening the door, threw her into the hallway. He shut the door and she began banging on it and cursing loudly. Elliot heard other guests yell at them to keep the noise down.

Finally, the banging and oaths subsided. He felt relieved that she had left, but his heart was pounding as he sat on the edge of his bed. She wasn't bad to look at, he mused, and he was somewhat flattered that she chose him. What the hell, she probably bedded down a dozen men before him. Too upset to sleep, he decided to go for a walk for a few minutes. After putting on his clothes, he silently descended the stairs and walked out into the crisp, cool night.

"Evening," a voice spoke out in the darkness.

Elliot jerked, then spun around, his gun drawn and cocked.

"Easy, friend, easy. What's your problem?"

"Who are you?" Elliot asked.

"I'm the deputy sheriff, mister. See the badge. Now put that iron away."

Noticing the badge, Elliot holstered his pistol. "Sorry, deputy, I guess I'm a little jumpy tonight."

"Say, you're pretty quick with that hog leg, stranger. How come you're so jumpy?"

"I guess I had too much to drink and couldn't sleep," Elliot lied.

"Uh huh. I just saw Jenny Mason storm out of the hotel in a huff. Wouldn't have anything to do with that, would it?" the deputy said.

Elliot felt ashamed. "Yeah," he replied reluctantly. "She wanted to do something I didn't want to do, if you know what I mean."

The deputy laughed. "Sure, I understand. She likes men, especially when Sonny leaves town. Say, wait a minute, stranger, did you turn her down?"

"Yeah, something like that."

"Miz Jenny don't take kindly to being spurned, stranger. From now on, if I was you, I'd steer clear of her. What's your name, anyway?"

"Elliot, Elliot Stewart."

Extending his hand, the deputy said, "My name's Foster Trent. I make my rounds about this time every night. Glad to know you."

"Deputy, I was asked to meet the sheriff here before I go back to the Lazy P ranch."

"Lazy P Ranch, huh? The sheriff's name is Tom Gentry and he pretty much cottons to the Lazy P bunch. If you want to meet him, he will be in the office around eight in the morning. You met that Senorita Paolo yet?"

"Yeah, nice lady," Elliot said.

"And a real looker, that one is," Foster said.

"By the way, deputy, do you know a Murtaugh here, a big fella?"

"You must mean Rusty Murtaugh. Yeah, a real headache, he and his brother Big Jim. But I heard Big Jim was killed a while ago, down around Fort Stockton way. Why?"

"Oh, nothing, someone just mentioned him. Well, I better try to get some sleep before the sun comes up. Good night, deputy," Elliot said, backing away.

The next morning, Elliot walked into the sheriff's office and introduced himself to Tom Gentry. They shook hands and the sheriff asked him to be seated.

"So, are you the man my deputy spoke to me about - meaning you and Jenny Mason?" Gentry asked.

"Yeah, I am," Elliot said, "but I don't want to mess around with no married woman, sheriff."

"Commendable, Mr. Stewart, but call me Tom. So, you're working for the Lazy P, eh? You planning on staying long?"

"I suppose so, Tom. Me and my partner have been on the trail a long time without a steady job. We kind of like to eat regular, you know."

"I understand. Senor Paolo is a good boss. You're lucky to have him. He don't hire many Americans so he must trust you pretty well."

"I suppose, sheriff," Elliot said. "I haven't known him long. He left for old Mexico just at the time he hired us."

"Us? You and your partner you mean, right?" Gentry inquired.

"Yessir, but there's another, too. Billy Carr is in town with us."

"Never heard of him," Tom pondered, stroking his chin. "So, when is senor Paolo due back or do you know?"

"No sir, I don't know," Elliot replied, looking out the window. "Oh, there's my partners now." He opened the door and hailed his companions.

Billy and Rafer entered and greeted the sheriff.

"I haven't seen them horses that you fellas brought in, but I heard about them," Gentry remarked

"Yeah, sheriff, them horses you got to see," Rafer said.

"Well, I suppose I'll have to make a special trip out there soon." He stared at Billy.

"Where're you from, son?"

"Originally, New Orleans, sheriff, why?"

"New Orleans, huh?"

"Sheriff, I ain't wanted nowhere. You can be sure of that. Oh, there might be a jealous husband or a mad father down the line somewheres," Billy said, grinning.

"Hell, if that was the case half the boys in this territory would be on the run," Gentry retorted, laughingly. "Anyway, glad to meet you boys. Give my best to Chavez."

"Right, sheriff," Rafer said and they departed.

"He seems to be a decent kind of fella," Elliot remarked. He was relieved that the sheriff hadn't mentioned Jenny in front of his friends. "Let's mount up, boys and head back to the ranch."

As the three men left town, Rafer and Billy talked about the whores they had the night before. They set an easy pace as both had headaches and were in no hurry to get to the ranch.

Elliot said nothing until the conversation got around to the poker game.

"I'll never know," Billy said, "why you let that loser call you a cheat."

"Me neither," Rafer added, "like Billy said, I'd have gut shot the S.O.B."

"Boys, it ain't worth killing a man over a few cards. Besides, I don't need a reputation around here. How would it look to Chavez and mister Paolo if I came to the ranch with blood on my hands?"

Elliot said, trying to roll a cigarette while on horseback.

"Just the same," Billy said, scratching himself, "I won't put up with that from nobody, and leaving all that money, mercy."

"So," Rafer said, "what we gonna do about that Murtaugh man, Elliot?"

"As far as I'm concerned," Elliot replied, "I'm staying clear of him. We got a good thing going here and I don't aim to spoil it."

"What are you two talking about?" Billy asked.

Rafer turned and explained the death of big Jim Murtaugh. Billy just shook his head and laughed.

Elliot slowed Toter down as he tried to roll a cigarette.

Then a man, crouching behind a pile of rocks, suddenly leaped out, brandishing a shotgun.

"Hold up, there!" the drygulcher demanded. He had a neckerchief covering his face.

Billy's horse shied, almost throwing him.

"Easy with that scatter gun, mister," Rafer said, holding his hands up. "We is poor wranglers. What you want with us anyways?"

Waving his shotgun back and forth, the waylayer said, "Give me your money, and no sudden moves, fellas."

"What makes you think we got any money?" Billy said.

"Do as I say and no back talk, hombres! I'd just as soon kill all of you and then pick your pockets. Now, make up your minds, what's it going to be? I ain't got all day."

Elliot stared at him. "Better do as he says, boys. He means it, and I don't aim to die over a few dollars"

They emptied their pockets and tossed the contents on the ground.

"Now, drop your gun belts easy like," the man demanded, "slowly and one at a time. I got an itchy trigger finger."

They let their gun belts fall, then tossed the rifles aside as well.

"Now move," the drygulcher yelled. "Get going, fast!"

The three spurred their mounts and rode away. Looking back, Elliot noticed the robber gather the money, but foolishly left the guns where they lay. Then he hurriedly mounted and sped away.

"Hold up, boys," Elliot said. "That idiot left our hardware." They turned their horses and returned, quickly dismounting and gathering their guns.

"I'm going after that hombre and get my money back," Billy said. "If he thinks for one minute that . . ."

"Forget it, Billy," Elliot declared, "I'm going after him alone. You two go on to the ranch and tell Chavez what happened. I won't be long because that fool didn't bother to change his clothes."

Rafer looked at him. "What do you mean?"

"Hell, didn't you notice?" Elliot said. "That was the guy that I hit over the head last night. Jim, remember?"

"Yeah, come to think of it, you're right," Billy said. "But he's got my money too, and I'll just go with you."

'It's only one man. He's my problem and I'll do it. Now, you guys go on," Elliot said, turning his mount. He began to follow the robber's spoor as Rafer and Billy headed again towards the ranch.

Not knowing the territory didn't bother him at all. He was determined to get the man. After all, he had left most of the money on the table because he wanted no more trouble. But this Jim had refused to leave well enough alone. Furthermore, he had also lifted Billy and Rafe's poke.

Elliot kicked his mare's flanks as he followed the tracks, which were very distinct and did not meander. He felt Jim knew exactly where he was headed. When Elliot happened across an old Indian, he stopped and asked him if he had seen a rider recently. The Indian nodded his head.

"Where does this trail lead, old one?" Elliot asked, pointing ahead of him.

"To place called Dry Wells," the Indian replied, shifting the load on his back.

"They got a sheriff there?"

"No lawmen. Bad place. Few white men. Few Navajo. Not good to go there, fair one."

'Thank you," Elliot said.

"Ho, fair one, you got tobacco?" the Indian said.

Elliot tossed him a small sack, thanked him, and spurred his horse. He felt that if he dogged this Jim closely, he wouldn't have time to spend their money.

Trash littered the road into Dry Wells as he rode in. He noticed one small store and several run-down clapboard shacks. A few were permanently boarded up. Elliot thought that if Jim had stopped here, he shouldn't be hard to find. The sun was quickly dropping out of sight and lanterns were turned up in some shacks. He noticed tethered horses in front of the lone store and headed toward it. He dismounted and checked the chamber of his pistol, reseating the weapon as he stepped gingerly onto a wooden sidewalk. He looked through the single dirty window and discerned several figures moving about inside. The sound of laughter filtered through the thin outer wall.

Elliot slowly entered and stood inside the door, scanning everyone present. He was satisfied that there were only four men here, the bartender and three seated around a rear table playing five card stud.

"Yessir, stranger," the bartender called, "come on in."

The seated men looked up.

"Barkeep," Elliot said, his eyes fixed on the seated gents, "get me a whiskey and as soon as I get my money, I'll pay you for it."

"Huh?" the bartender said, hesitating in the middle of filling a glass.

Elliot headed toward the table. He immediately recognized the man called Jim, who, in turn stiffened at the sight of him.

"You got something that belongs to me, Jim."

"I don't know what you're talking about, stranger," Jim said, avoiding Elliot's stare.

"You don't, eh? I tell you what. You empty your pockets on the table and if you ain't got close to a hundred dollars in your poke, I'll let you go. How about it?"

"Hey, you fellas is my witness," the robber blurted out, "he's trying to steal my money."

"It ain't your money and you know it. Now, what's it gonna be?" Elliot said, shifting on his left leg, a sure sign that he was ready to draw. His right arm hung loosely down his side.

Jim's two table companions looked at one another, then slowly rose and backed away.

The cocking of a gun behind him alerted Elliot to danger. He looked around and saw the bartender with a shotgun.

"Mister," Elliot said cooly, "if you make one more stupid move with that scatter gun, you better have a will made out."

The bartender looked at him, then Jim, and slowly replaced the shotgun under the counter.

Out of the corner of his eye, Elliot noticed that Jim, still seated at the table, was making his move. Knowing that it was difficult to draw a bolstered pistol while seated, Elliot turned and immediately his gun jumped in his hand and blue smoke ejected from the barrel. Jim's body jerked backward, slamming against the wall. Crimson blood rapidly spread across his chest as he looked down, bewildered and frightened. Then slowly, he sank down the wall, clutching his breast.

Elliot moved toward his victim and kneeled. "Damn it, man, why'd you take my money after I left plenty on the table? You brought this on yourself, you know."

Coughing up blood, the robber whispered, "It was Jenny, man. Jenny gave me twenty dollars to drygulch you."

"Jenny? You mean Jenny Mason?"

"Yeah, Jenny. She said you had it coming," Jim said, his voice faltering.

"Damn her anyway," Elliot gasped. "She had no call to do that to either of us."

Jim did not respond. Elliot reached over and closed the dead man's eyes. Then he slowly got up, pocketed the retrieved money, and retreated to the bar.

"I'll take that drink now," Elliot said, shaking. He downed it slowly as the bartender stepped back, "and a chaw of tobacco."

The barkeep turned and nervously fingered some wrapped tobacco off the shelf. Elliot pulled out a few bills and scattered them on the table.

"Give that poor hombre a decent burial, will you?" Elliot said.

"If you don't mind my asking, mister," the bartender said, "just what is your name?"

Elliot started for the door, then turned. "I do mind, because you ain't never going to see me again, not in this one-horse town anyway."

Mounting, he started for the Lazy P.

Silently, he cursed Jenny Mason for setting him up. Deputy Trent was correct, she couldn't take no for an answer. He hoped this would be the end of it.

It was cool as he sank deeper into his parka.

8

Elliot made the long trek back to the ranch through the night. It was late and everyone was asleep as he collapsed in bed, bone tired.

Almost immediately, it seemed, he heard the clang of the breakfast alarm. He got up and hurriedly dressed.

Flapjacks, slab bacon, hominy, and hot coffee were set before the wranglers. Billy took a seat next to Elliot and held out his hand. Grinning, Elliot dug in his pocket for Billy's money.

"Did you kill him?" Billy asked, raising a coffee cup to his lips.

"Naw, I didn't," Elliot replied, calmly. "No call to."

"No call to? You mean to tell me that you caught up to him and he just handed the money over to you, no fuss?"

"Nope, no fuss," Elliot whispered, stuffing bacon into his mouth.

"Well, I'll just be damned," Billy said, turning to Rafer. "If that don't beat all, Rafe"

Rafer just grinned and poured more syrup on his flapjacks.

As Billy continued to talk loudly to Rafer, Elliot had no choice but to listen in.

"I'd just as soon killed that drygulcher, myself," Billy remarked.

"So what makes you think he ain't dead?" Rafer whispered.

"Well, Elliot said ..."

"Hell, Billy, he ain't gonna tell you the truth anyway," Rafer responded, "but I'll bet you a month's wages, me and you will never see that drygulcher again."

Billy looked at Elliot then back to Rafer and shook his head. "Is he pretty good with a six-shooter?" Billy asked Rafer, while raising his coffee again.

"He ain't bad. Nope, he ain't bad at all. Now pass some more of that there bacon and tell Elliot I want my money too."

With breakfast over, they gathered outside and Elliot rolled a cigarette. Huddling close because of the chilled air, they listened while Chavez gave each wrangler his daily work instructions. As the group broke up to begin their chores, Elliot saw Senorita Paolo standing outside the house. She wore a full-length dark dress with a rebozo draped over her shoulders and arms. Her dark hair slightly flared in the soft morning breeze.

Rafer looked at her and whispered, "Elliot, I swear she's staring a hole right through you."

Glancing at Rafer, Elliot said, "C'mon, partner, we got to mend fences."

They mounted their horses and rode to the western part of the ranch. Donning gloves, they began repairing the fences, removing damaged wire and replacing it with new, using stretchers and then nailing the strands tight. As the day progressed, Elliot removed his coat, and cutting a wad of tobacco, continued. Later, they rode to the north, checking and repairing the seemingly endless fence line.

Finally, satisfied they had done a good day's work, they rested.

"This ain't bad country, is it?" Rafer said.

"No, partner, it ain't bad at all," Elliot replied. "At least we got jobs and eat regular. It's been a right smart while since we could say that."

"You remember when we left the troop in '65? That time we were coming through Arkansas?" Rafer said.

"What about it?"

"When we stopped at that old farmer's place and asked for something to eat?"

"So?"

"Do you remember his daughter that was there? She was a real pretty little thing, milking them cows and toting that bucket of milk all the way to the house. Well, I want you to know she made eyes at me. Me, a cripple and all. I never did tell you about it but we got together that night."

"Are you telling me that you bedded her down, on her own place?" Elliot inquired, rolling a cigarette. "It's a wonder her pa didn't find out and clear us out with buckshot, Rafe."

"I know but she sure was a sweet thing. If me and you hadn't kept going, as partners, I'd have married that filly," Rafer confessed.

"And done what? Stayed on that rundown farm and milked cows for the rest of your life?"

"So, what have we had in the meantime? We ain't exactly been getting rich these past ten years."

Elliot rolled another cigarette and tossed the empty sack aside.

Rafer laid back and cocked his hat low over his face.

"What are you gonna do when that senorita starts making eyes at you?" Rafer asked.

"Hell, Rafe, didn't you hear Chavez? She's gonna marry a Spaniard from Mexico."

"I knowed what was said, Elliot, but I want an answer," Rafer said, raising and looking him straight in the eye.

"I don't hanker on making my boss mad for sure," Elliot responded, "and I surely don't want to lose my job."

"Then I suppose that means you ain't gonna have nothing to do with her, right?"

"Right. Look, she's class folk. Her pa's rich and promised her to someone else. I got as much chance with her as I have the Queen of England. Still, she is a beautiful woman," he said, smiling.

"You said a mouthful, man."

"Well, c'mon, Rafe," Elliot said, "let's finish up and head back to the ranch. It'll be dark soon, and I don't want to miss supper." He tossed the cigarette aside.

Jumping up. Rafe went directly to his horse. "That's the best thing you've said all day, partner."

The ranch was quiet when they arrived back at dark. Most of the hands were already in the cookhouse eating. Quickly washing up, the two joined them. After eating, the hands gathered in front of the bunk-house and talked.

"Winter will soon be here, amigos, "Jose Estavez said, "and the snows will come. I don't like the cold or the snow."

"I don't know of nobody that does," Rafer countered. "When the cold comes, my leg bothers me something awful."

Elliot got up momentarily and went in the bunkhouse for his coat. Billy greeted him upon his return. "I guess you and Rafer will be staying on," he said.

"I suppose. Why?" Elliot said, sitting.

"Well, I was kind of hankering to go to California in the spring."

"Well, I hear California is nice," Rafer said.

"Senor Stewart."

Elliot jerked upright and saw Senorita Paolo standing in the shad-ows. The three of them stood up, Billy taking off his bowler.

"Senorita," Elliot said, "you scared the fire out of me."

"I'm sorry, gentlemen, I did not mean to frighten you," she said, stepping into the light.

After staring at each other for a moment, Billy excused himself, as did Rafer, and they went into the bunkhouse.

Elliot, dumbstruck, found it difficult to talk.

"Maybe, I should go in, too," he remarked.

"Please, walk with me for a moment," she said, wrapping her shawl closer over her arms to counter the chill.

"Well, ma'am, I don't want to bother you none," he said ner-vously.

"Come," she said and he obediently followed.

"Do you like to work here, Elliot?"

"Yes, ma'am, I do," he replied.

"I would like for you to call me Maria, Elliot."

"Well, I don't feel comfortable calling you by your first name. It don't feel right, you being the boss's daughter and all," he stammered.

"The boss's daughter, you say." She laughed. "Yes, as you say, I am the boss's daughter, and because of it, I am lonely. Everyone places me in an untouchable position and I find it offensive. Can you under-stand that?"

"Well, I suppose so ..."

"Elliot, I am a woman, am I not?"

"Well, yes, you certainly are," he said as they stepped on the porch of the house.

"Do you find me attractive?" she said, running her hand through her hair.

"You know damn good and well you are. More like beautiful."

"Thank you, Elliot. It is always refreshing for a woman to hear that," she said, gazing deeply into his eyes. He looked away.

"Why do you not look at me?"

He thrust his hands in his back pockets and nervously shifted. His legs felt like jelly.

"Miss Maria, I, I don't feel right being here talking to you," he said.

Sensing his feelings, she said, "It is late, Elliot, and I'm keeping you from your sleep. Thank you for walking with me. Good night." She turned and Elliot noticed Consuelo looking out the window at the two. Passing, Maria stuck her tongue out at the housekeeper, who, mortified at this gesture, turned away. Maria smiled.

Elliot walked slowly toward the bunkhouse, his head swimming as he fantasized making love to this gorgeous creature.

Stepping out of the shadows, Rafer confronted him. "Well?"

"Well, what?" Elliot said.

"Now, Elliot, you're gonna get yourself in trouble fooling around with that young'n and you know it," Rafer declared, "and if you get in trouble, then I'm gonna be in trouble, too."

"Partner, I'm sorry, I don't want to get nobody in trouble, but, damn, she's so good looking and all."

"What you need to do is get it out of your system," Rafe said, "and go to Las Cruces and get you one of them whores."

Elliot laughed as they entered the bunkhouse.

Rafer, laying on his bunk, mused that Elliot could jeopardize their remaining on the ranch. If he made a move towards the Senorita and her pa finds out, they would be kicked off the place. He was worried thinking he could lose the best job he's had in years. Elliot had no right to do this to him.

The next day Chavez gathered the men and informed them they were to brand the horses. Elliot was loath to put a mark on these beautiful animals but a brand was necessary.

However, Chavez produced a branding iron with a small Lazy P. This appeared to Elliot as acceptable. But when it was the black stallion's turn to be marked, Elliot turned away when the horse shrieked in pain.

When Senor Paolo returned, he would ask him if he would sell the stallion to him. He loved Toter but she was getting a little old. He doubted if he could afford the stallion, but he would never know if he didn't ask.

It took most of the day to brand the horses and after finishing, the wranglers bathed in the cold, stagnant water of the cow pond.

A young, Mexican girl from the house came to pick up their stinking clothes. She would place them in hot, soapy water and scrub them. The wranglers appreciated this gesture.

Rafer took a liking to her immediately. She was somewhat attractive, thin with long, jet black hair and a ready smile. Her name was Juanita and looked to be about seventeen years of age. She was Consuelo's niece.

When she had returned with the clean, folded jeans and shirts, Billy had gently patted her on the rear. Noticing, Rafer took exception to this and admonished Billy in front of Juanita. She smiled at Rafer thinking that she had a champion. Billy saw this gesture and laughed heartily, full knowing that he had done Rafer a good turn.

For the next few days, the ranch hands were busy gathering supplies to be transported to the distant line cabins. Wagons filled with food, tobacco, tools, heavy clothing, blankets, and water casks were readied. This territory, although dry and dusty during the summer, produced heavy snows, often with hail, during the winter.

Stationing the ranch hands in the line cabins reduced the movement time for them to check the cattle and sheep. Besides, there was little to do with so many hands around the ranch proper.

Leaving Billy at the ranch, Elliot and Rafer went on horseback, accompanying Jose, who drove one of the wagons. They had only gone a few miles when they found the remains of a butchered steer. Climbing down from the wagon, Jose knelt and examined the carcass as Elliot and Rafer looked around.

"Mescalero," Jose said. "Do you see the broken arrow there? They take everything, sometimes even the bones, always the insides!"

"And they don't even cut the fence," Rafer remarked.

"No, they don't wish to make trouble for us," Jose said, getting up.

"Well, I'm sure glad you fellas got a understanding with them redskins," Rafer said, smiling, "because I don't hanker no problems with them."

"Si, Rafer, my friend," Jose said, mounting, "it has been this way for many years." He slapped the team reins and the wagon continued.

"Jose, that girl, Juanita - she belong to anyone?" Rafer asked.

"No, senor, she does not. Do you like her?"

"Well, sort of. Don't you think she's pretty?"

"Yes, she is, senor."

Listening, Elliot smiled to himself.

They had gone about a mile when gunshots echoed in the distance. Reining up, Elliot looked at Jose. "What's going on?" he shouted.

"I don't know, but I don't like the sound of it," Jose said. "It is on our range."

"Leave the wagon, Jose," Elliot yelled. "Get on my horse, and let's take a look."

Rafer had already spurred his cayuse toward the noise.

Topping a sandy knoll, Elliot saw puffs of smoke in the valley below, His mind raced as he squinted his eyes, trying to determine who was shooting at who. He stood up in his stirrups as Jose looked around him.

There were many men below them running along a dry creek bed.

"Comancheros," Jose muttered.

"Who are those people in the rocks above them?"

Jose pointed. 'That one is my wife's brother, Carlos, and there is Manuel next to him."

"Rafe," Elliot shouted, "you take the high ground to the right and I'll take the left. We'll catch them in a crossfire. Get down, Jose."

Jose jumped off the mare and Elliot dug hard into Toter's flank. The wild-eyed mare lunged forward. Circling the desperados, he sought a place to stop. Spotting a thick-trunked bristlecone pine, he unsheathed his rifle and leaped behind the short tree.

Sweat was pouring off his face and his heart pounded heavily as he cocked the rifle. A shot passed closely over his head as he attempted to see through the dust. Wiping his eyes, he focused on a fat, squat Mexican sporting loose tan leggings, who was running across a clearing. Licking his dry lips, Elliot leveled the Winchester's buckhorn sights on the figure. Squeezing the trigger, the gun roared, but the distant figure moved at the same time. Seeing his slug kick up dust behind the man, he re-cocked and again pulled the trigger. A second later, the man threw up his hands and fell headlong into the brush.

Dust immediately flew up at Elliot's heels. Someone now had him in his sights. He tried to squeeze even closer to the tree. Fleetingly, his mind raced back to Dunkers Church and the cornfield at Antietam. The rushing Blue bellies were mercilessly cut down by the withering rebel fire. He had cried while recharging his muzzle loader. The carnage was complete even as the Yankees momentarily retreated through the mangled cornfield.

Elliot shook his head as a huge form rushed at him. As he rolled out of the way, he saw a raised machete wielded by a dark-skinned brute of a man. The machete caught him high on the arm, slicing deep, but at the moment, he did not feel the pain. His mind was too occupied to pay attention to his nerves.

Elliot threw dust at the charging Mex, hoping to blind him momentarily until he could clear his single action pistol. He rolled again in the blinding dust as he instinctively pointed his weapon and pulled the trigger. The bullet caught the charging hulk along the teeth line and the back of his head exploded. The man fell on top of Elliot, knocking him out of breath for a second. Rolling the sweating, stinking man off of him, Elliot sat up, coughing to regain his breath. Looking at the corpse, he saw the dark red blood quickly staining the ground. Whew, he thought, this mountain of a man hadn't bathed in years.

Sitting up, he noticed the firing had stopped. It was then he felt the blood trickle within his torn, new shirt. Finally, the pain had arrived. Hurriedly taking his neckerchief off, he wrapped it around his arm.

Jose rushed to him. "Senor Stewart, are you all right?"

"Yeah," Elliot replied, "have you seen Rafe?"

Spitting on the dead form, Jose replied, "Si, he is all right, but Manuel, he is dead."

"I'm sorry, Jose. How many of them were there?" Elliot asked.

"I think seven, Elliot, but I'm not sure. Two of them got away."

Standing up, Elliot leaned over and retrieved his rifle. "Well, we need to get back to the buckboard, Jose. Get one of them ponies down there and we'll put Manuel on it and take him home."

As Elliot sat down on the ground away from the dead Mexican, Rafer rode up.

"You hurt bad, partner?" Rafe inquired.

"Naw, but the supplies to the line cabin will have to wait, Rafe. I got to get this arm sewed up."

"I gotcha, Elliot," Rafe said, "let's go."

"But, amigo," Jose said, glancing around, "what of the dead ones? They need a Christian burial."

"Them's wasn't Christians, Jose," Elliot said, grimacing. "And as for burial, we ain't got near the time them vultures have got."

Rafer brought his pony over and held out the reins. They rode over and helped Jose place Manuel's body across the horse. Then they slowly returned to the ranch.

Seeing the trio returning, Chavez rode out to greet them.

"You are hurt, Elliot," he said. "What happened?"

"It was Comancheros. We beat them good," Jose remarked, "but Manuel is dead, Chavez."

"Jose, take Manuel to his family. Come, Elliot, we must dress that wound," Chavez said, gesturing toward the house.

While the two were walking, Chavez yelled for Consuelo, who soon came out, wiping her hands on her apron. Seeing the wounded Elliot, she ran to help him. As they entered the house, Elliot blushed as Maria joined them with a concerned look.

Consuelo unraveled the neckerchief and gasped.

"Senor, it is a deep wound and it must be sewed together to heal," she said.

"I will do it, Consuelo," Maria commanded. "Bring fresh bandages and alcohol. Chavez, bring some cognac."

Chavez turned to do her bidding while Maria directed Elliot to sit down. She told Rafer to wait outside as there were enough attendees.

Chavez, returning, handed Elliot a hefty tumbler of cognac and urged him to drink it quickly.

Elliot grimaced as Maria doused the wound with alcohol. He took another drink of cognac. It burned going down but was delicious. He was pretty drunk by the time Maria began closing the wound. Stepping back, she admonished Elliot for putting his life in danger. As he began to explain, he noticed tears in her dark eyes.

"Why must men try to prove their manhood by killing others and they themselves may die?" she said.

"But, Maria," Elliot said consolingly, "it wasn't my fault. What was I supposed to do? I can't run and let your people suffer. I don't look for no trouble, but it's hard trying to stay out of trouble in this country."

"You are right, of course. I am sorry for what I said. We should be grateful for what you did." She looked at him with pain on her face. "Now," she continued, finishing the bandage, "you must get some rest."

"Yes, ma'am," Elliot said docilely. "Whatever you say, but can I have another swig of that cognac first?"

Maria laughed, as did Chavez, who poured him another drink.

Later, Elliot, with his arm in a sling, walked outside and saw Rafer and Billy talking with the other wranglers.

"And you should've seen this one coming at me," Rafer was saying. "He was ahollering and shooting on the run, but he couldn't hit the side of a barn. I dropped him with one shot in the belly. Hey, Elliot, how many of them hombres did you get?"

"Rafe, I was so busy, I didn't have time to count," Elliot replied. "Hell, I'm just lucky I wasn't killed."

Turning back to the others, Rafer continued with his recollection of the event plus a little exaggeration.

Elliot unsteadily made his way to the bunkhouse and wearily collapsed on his bunk. Before falling asleep, he thought about the tears in Maria's eyes. She was so young and beautiful and had bravely sewed his arm without so much as a twitch.

For the next three days, Elliot was on the mend, watching others as they loaded wagons with the necessary supplies and moved off toward the distant cabins. Feeling somewhat useless, he at times, tried to gather wood for the cook's fires. However, Chavez berated him, saying that his wound would reopen and never heal properly. Maria scolded him also. Several times she came to check the condition of his arm and change the bandage, but being in the bunkhouse together made Elliot uncomfortable in her presence.

While attending to him, she would be aware that his eyes were upon her and when she looked up he would avoid her eyes.

One day a buckboard drove up and Elliot saw Maria greet the occupants, who climbed down and entered the house while chatting with her.

"Jose, who are those people?" Elliot asked.

"That is Senor Frank Simpson, his wife and daughter, amigo. They are our neighbors to the north. Our patron is very fond of Mr. Simpson."

"Mr. Simpson's wife is a very pretty woman," Elliot said, staring.

"Yes, she is much younger than he, amigo. She is from back east, a place called Saint Louis."

At dark, the visitors walked out of the house and Elliot saw Maria hug Mrs. Simpson and her daughter. Then the visitors climbed on the buckboard and left the ranch.

Maria spotted Elliot and sauntered over to him. "And how is your arm today?"

"Oh, it's coming along nicely," he said.

She gestured toward the departing Simpsons.

"They own a small ranch to our north," Maria said. "They are good people. Mister Simpson said that a few of our cattle had strayed onto his range and he did not have enough hands to round them up. I will have Chavez to go there and bring them back."

"Must be a hole in the fence somewhere," Elliot said.

"Jose, please find Chavez and bring him to me," she commanded.

Without a word, he left to find Chavez.

"The young one is Carol. One day she will become a beautiful woman," Maria said, "like her mother. Her father is quite fond of her."

"I can see why," he said.

"Mr. Simpson also told me that there seemed to be a lot of comanchero activity to the north and east of his place," Maria said, "and I do not like that. I only wish my father were here. He would know what to do."

Elliot slipped his sling off and began to work his hands and shoulders.

"Elliot, you should let the bandages remain awhile longer to completely heal."

Elliot smiled. "It's feeling much better Maria, and besides, I can't earn my pay walking around hobbled like this."

Chavez came to her. "Senorita, you sent for me?"

She told him of the stray cattle. Chavez nodded quickly and turned to leave.

"Chavez," Elliot said, grabbing his arm, "can I go with you?"

"Si, and tell Billy I want him as well."

Elliot touched his hat to Maria as he turned toward the corral.

Saddling up, Chavez led a group of five ranch hands northward, where they met Frank Simpson, who showed them where there was a break in the fence. They rounded up the Lazy P strays and ran them through the fence, then began repairing the damaged portion.

When they were finished, they decided to stay at one of the line cabins. Frank Simpson, together with his daughter, rode up in a buckboard. They had brought food for the Lazy P wranglers, and that evening they ate well and talked.

Frank Simpson sat next to Chavez, pulled out his pipe, filled it with tobacco and lit it.

"Listen, Chavez, have you heard anything about a large bunch of Comancheros that have been seen east of us?

"No, I haven't, Frank."

"Seems they had come out of Texas with Rangers and yellow legs on their tail. You know, of course, we can't afford to have them near us. I'd hate to think about..."

"Yeah, anyway Frank," Chavez said quietly, "we'll keep a lookout for them, and if either one of us hears anything, the other will find out. Right?"

"Good enough, my friend."

Billy was watching young Carol wash the dishes. Her ribboned blue and white frock reached to her ankles. Her golden hair fell loosely about her shoulders. Billy surmised she couldn't be more than fourteen although a real beauty. Finishing up, she turned and smiled at him.

"Poppa, I'm done," she called.

"Okay, honey. We'll go in a few minutes,"

Elliot kept his eyes on Billy, who had not even noticed his presence. It was amusing to Elliot.

"That maverick, Sonny Mason, wanted to buy my ranch," Simpson revealed.

At the mention of Mason, Elliot perked up.

"Oh, he was willing to pay top dollar, almost fifteen an acre, but hell, I don't need his money," Simpson continued, "and I'm sure you don't need him as a neighbor."

"No, I do not really like him," Chavez said, "let him stay in town and mind his own business. Besides, what does he know of raising cattle?"

Simpson laughed and nodded. Emptying his pipe bowl on the floor, he rose.

"Well, it's getting late, fellas and we need to skedaddle on home. Carol, honey, let's go."

Billy jumped up and opened the door for them. She smiled at him as she walked through but Frank merely frowned.

Elliot thought that one day she will be a real heartbreaker, for sure.

The buckboard left as Chavez thanked them both and waved.

9

Gunshots and the rush of wranglers toward the ranch gate heralded Senor Paolo's arrival. When the buckboard stopped, Maria rushed out and kissed her father. Then he turned to meet the others. The wranglers took off their hats and sombreros as he walked among them and shook their hands.

Elliot, his arm completely healed, walked up and took his turn.

"Senor Stewart, it is good to see you again," Paolo said. "Chavez has told me of what you and Senor Summers have done. I am indebted to you both. I am also glad that you decided to stay with us. Tell me, do you like it here?"

"Yessir, it's a fine place to work, thank you."

"So, stay with me a moment," Paolo said, and turned to the crowd. In a loud voice, he announced, "We will have a feast this evening for my safe return. Vaqueros, will you join me?"

The men raised their voices in the affirmative.

Then, taking Maria by the hand, Paolo gestured for Elliot to join them in the house. Chavez followed closely.

Inside, Paolo pulled a decanter of wine from a drawer and began pouring drinks. He asked about the recent comanchero battle and the conditions of the thoroughbreds. Chavez turned his eyes downward when he informed his patron that they had lost two of the prized animals. Placing his hands on Chavez's shoulder, Paolo said in a low voice, "My companion, it is no fault of yours, I know. You did all you could. Now, hold up your head, finish your drink, and see that the others prepare for the feast tonight."

Chavez, relieved of his responsibility, quickly downed his drink and departed.

Paolo then turned to Elliot, smiling. "Tonight we celebrate, my friend. The Mexican loves to eat and to dance, especially to dance. They work hard and are poor, but they love a fiesta, this you will see." He refilled Elliot's glass. The wine was a pale red and fruity, too sweet for Elliot's palate, but he drank it all.

Maria accompanied him to the door, smiled and then returned to her father's side.

"I missed you, father," Elliot heard her say. "Please do not be gone for so long again."

Paolo laughed, "Maria, my dear, I trust you to see that the cooks, Consuelo, Juanita and the other household staff prepare a grand meal to celebrate my return. Now, it has been a long journey, and I am tired. I wish to rest for a little while."

"Certainly, Consuelo and I will take care of everything."

"Thank you," he said and left.

That evening, Elliot heard the Mexican string quartet begin playing as he was still readying himself for the festivities. The bunkhouse was empty as he brushed his teeth and combed his hair. Walking out, he met Harry Two-Horse, and the two walked together.

"Elliot, I must tell you that it is customary that the patron should dance the first dance with his daughter. No one else must begin dancing until he finishes," Harry said.

"Oh, I didn't know that, but it's good you told me, Harry. Thanks."

Elliot noticed that covered lanterns were hung from the cottonwood trees. Many tables, resplendent with starched, embroidered tablecloths, were placed everywhere, complete with bottles of tequila. He saw a large fire, atop of which was a spitted quarter beef, turning slowly.

The cowboys were already drinking heavily, but all waited until Paolo made his entrance. Elliot also saw that Rafer, turning up a bottle and whooping, probably would not last long.

In a few moments, Paolo appeared with Maria holding his arm. They walked straight to the dance floor and whirled to the music. Elliot felt good that Maria was laughing and enjoying herself. She looked over at him several times. Then tiring, Paolo squired Maria to one of the tables.

The others quickly flowed onto the dance floor.

Maria came to Elliot and asked him to grace their table. As they were approaching, Elliot saw the Simpson family walk up. Paolo stood up and embraced all three of the Simpsons.

Rafer was dancing with a huge, buxomly Mexican woman and coming nearer, he shouted for Elliot to dance. Elliot just smiled and shook his head.

Paolo stood up and held his hand out to the Simpson daughter. She smiled and went to the dance floor with him. The Simpsons also smiled and lifted their wine glasses to the dancing duo.

Turning to Maria, Elliot said, "Everybody seems to be having a good time."

"Why don't you dance, Elliot? There are many lovely women here."

"It ain't that, ma'am. I ain't never really learned how to dance. Not that way anyway," Elliot confessed, staring at the dancers' feet.

"If you like, I can teach you. It is quite easy."

"Maybe some other time, Maria. I got two left feet and tonight I would just look silly."

Rafer saw Juanita walking along the perimeter of the dance floor. He immediately left his partner and moved unsteadily towards her.

"Please, young lady, will you dance with me," he said.

Juanita, shy, cast her eyes down and smiled.

"I sure would like you to dance with me because you sure are pretty, Juanita."

She looked at him and held out her hand.

Rafer whooped and squired her to the floor.

Elliot said, "He is going to have one whale of a headache come morning."

"Yes, but tonight he is having fun, is he not?" Maria said. "Come, it is cool. Let us move closer to the fire."

They moved toward the blaze just as Rafer fell down almost pulling Juanita with him. Everyone roared and Rafer was helped up. He resumed dancing.

As they reached the warmth of the fire, Elliot looked back and saw someone familiar approaching their table.

"I know him," Elliot said, as Maria followed his eyes, "Sonny Mason, ain't it?"

"Oh yes, he owns a saloon in Las Cruces. He is a friend to my father."

"Yeah, Sonny Mason," Elliot said, as she looked up at him, "his wife's named Jenny."

'You know of his wife?"

"Sort of," Elliot said, blushing a little, "I've seen her in his saloon."

"I've heard she can be a real she-cat," she said.

Elliot noticed that Mason was talking to Mr. Simpson, who appeared annoyed at the intrusion. A few moments later, Paolo, who had been making the rounds of greeting people, joined them. Elliot did not see Jenny Mason, and decided Sonny must have come by himself. Good, he thought. He wouldn't have felt comfortable had she shown up.

Chavez walked up with a bottle of tequila and filled his glass.

"Whoa, let up, partner," Elliot said. "That stuffs mean."

"But it is this one night to celebrate, Elliot," Chavez retorted, turning and moving on.

As the hour grew late, the wranglers, mostly drunk, began to take leave. Paolo sauntered up to the twosome.

"It is late, Maria, and I am tired. I will say my goodnights to everyone and go to bed. Elliot, my friend, I will see you tomorrow."

Paolo placed his small hand on Elliot's arm.

"Good night, senor, and thank you for a wonderful party," Elliot commented.

As Paolo moved away, Elliot followed him with his eyes.

"You are a very lucky woman," he said, "to have such a fine father."

"Yes, I am. It is a shame that he is alone, not having my mother with him. They were very devoted to each other. Well, in a moment,

I must leave as well. I will have a busy day tomorrow cleaning up this mess." Maria sighed.

Elliot noticed that Sonny Mason had already departed and the Simpsons also readied to leave.

Then he saw that Rafer had passed out, and that Harry and Jose were attempting to pick him up. He hurried over and helped them as they shuttled Rafer to the bunkhouse. They all laughed when they saw the grin on Rafer's face. Then Elliot turned to see Maria following them.

They threw Rafer on his bunk and Elliot pulled a blanket over the prostrate form.

Then he hurried back outside and found Maria lingering near the door.

"Well, Maria, it's getting late," he whispered, "and I guess I'd better turn in myself." The tequila had made him a little light-headed, but he felt good.

"Before you go in, would you see me to the house?" she asked.

"Sure, I'd be glad to." Slowly, they walked until at the door, she turned and gazed up at him.

"Well," he said, "good night, Maria ..."

"Do you not want to kiss me, Elliot?"

The sweet smell of jasmine made his senses numb, that and the tequila. He started to kiss her as she leaned forward, her eyes half closed. Then he pulled back.

"No, m'am. I can't do this."

She looked at him hesitatingly, and took one step backward. He saw the anger sweep across her face, then she whirled and left.

"Oh boy, did you mess up there."

Elliot turned to be confronted with Billy.

"You're a damn fool, Elliot. I would've certainly taken advantage of a kiss with that one."

"You ain't me, Billy," he said, moving past Billy into the bunkhouse.

Chuckling, Billy followed him in.

Devon Mitchell was in Mason's Bar, having a drink, when Sonny walked by. "Hey, Mr. Mason," he said, "Could I talk to you a minute?" Sonny slowly came over and sat down.

"Look, I need a job, Mr. Mason. Do you know of anyone that I could talk to? I'm good with horses and cattle, but I don't plow ground."

"Didn't I hear somewhere that you worked for the Lazy P, bringing those thoroughbreds up from Fort Stockton?" Sonny inquired.

"Yeah, I did."

"So why didn't you stay on with them?"

"Well, I was going north, but I stayed here too long and now my money's gone," Devon lamented.

"I see," Sonny said, rubbing his chin. "Have you tried the Simpson spread?"

"Yeah, I spoke to Mr. Simpson, but he couldn't use me."

"I tell you what," Sonny said, "you stick around and maybe I can get something for you."

"But, Mr. Mason, I'm broke, I tell you."

Reaching in his pocket, Sonny extracted a few bills. "Here," he said, "take this. I'll stake you until we can find something for you."

"Thanks, Mr. Mason, I appreciate this," Devon replied, fingering the bills.

Sonny stood up and went to his office.

"Barkeep, bring me another drink," Devon shouted, turning around. He was surprised to see a big man standing at his table.

"What do you want?" Devon asked, feeling agitated at this intrusion.

"My name's Murtaugh, Mitchell, and I seen you around town. Mind if I set down?"

"Suit yourself," Devon said, taking the drink from the bartender.

"I'm looking for a man by the name of Elliot something-or-other," Murtaugh said.

"So?"

"I need to find him. Have you heard of this gent?"

"I know an Elliot, but what do you want him for, mister?" Devon asked.

"I owe him something, Mitchell, and I need to get it to him as soon as I can. So, where can I find him?"

"What's it worth to you, Murtaugh?" Devon asked, glaring at him.

Rusty Murtaugh reached in his poke and pulled out a ten-dollar gold piece. Placing it on the table, he stared at Devon. Devon reached over to pick it up, but Murtaugh put his hand over Devon's and waited for a reply.

"There's an Elliot Stewart working at the Lazy P right now. That's the only Elliot I know," Devon said. Rusty raised his hand, releasing the coin, then he stood up. "Thanks," Murtaugh whispered, then turned and walked out. Devon raised the glass to his lips.

10

"Senor," Consuelo announced, "Mr. Mason to see you."

Paolo got up as Sonny hurried past the maid.

"Welcome, my friend," Paolo cried, shaking his hand vigorously. "Please come in and sit. Consuelo, please bring some cognac."

"So, Senor Mason, you grace my humble casa. To what do I owe this pleasure/"

"Senor, I came to ask a favor of you," Sonny said, smiling.

"If it is in my power to grant it, Mr. Mason, then I will, gladly," Paolo remarked.

Consuelo returned with a decanter and two glasses. Paolo poured a small glass with dark cognac and handed it to Sonny, then poured another for himself.

"Salut, my friend," Paolo said, raising his glass. Sonny responded.

"Senor, a few days ago," Sonny began, "I went to Frank Simpson and asked him to sell me some of his land. Between you and him, most of the good land hereabout is taken up."

"I see," Paolo said, "and . . . ?"

"Well, he practically kicked me off his place and quite frankly, I didn't deserve it."

"Yes, Frank can be headstrong at times, my friend. I'm sorry."

"Well, I would like to buy some land, and I'm willing to pay top dollar, too," Sonny continued.

"Perhaps you might talk to the H Bar H outfit over to the east, Mr. Mason," Paolo said, raising his glass again.

"You and I both know that place ain't fit for raising cattle, senor," Sonny said, fidgeting uncomfortably. "So, I'm asking you, sir. Would you sell me some of your land?"

"This land? Oh no, my friend, that is impossible. This is home to many old friends and I could not, in good faith to them and my departed wife, part with any of it. I'm sorry, but I'm sure that you can understand," Paolo said.

"But, senor, you have so much, sure —"

Paolo shook his head. "I'm sorry, my friend, but no." Paolo said.

"If you ever decide to sell any of it, I wish that you would inform me, senor," Sonny said, finishing his cognac. He stood up to leave.

"Must you leave so soon, my friend?"

"Yes, I need to get back to my business."

They walked outside together and Sonny spotted the thoroughbreds in the corral as he reached his horse.

"Senor, your horses are beautiful."

"They are, aren't they?" Paolo said, gazing at the animals.

Without another word, Sonny mounted, turned and rode off. A moment later, Chavez walked up.

"Patron," he said, "what did the gringo want?"

"He wanted to buy some of our land," Paolo said, smiling.

"What? That gringo had the nerve to ask you that?" Chavez said, disbelievingly.

Paolo laughed. "Chavez, don't hold it against him. He has a right to ask. No harm done."

The cold northwest wind was heralding the first sign of winter with snow flurries. All of the supplies had been delivered to the line cabins and very soon the ranch hands would be split up to occupy the cabins until spring.

Elliot was in the stable one evening, brushing and feeding hay to his mare, when Maria walked in.

"Why, hello," he said, 'It's pretty cold out, ain't it?"

"Yes, it is," she replied, walking up and stroking his horse. He continued brushing.

"Why do you deliberately avoid me, Elliot?" she asked. "You said that I was desirable and ..."

Elliot ceased brushing Toter and looked at her. "Maria, it wouldn't be right. What with me, a no-nothing cowhand and you to marry some other man. I got no money ~ nothing."

She placed her hand on his arm. "That is not a good enough answer to suit me."

"Plus the fact, young lady, I stand to lose my job. Chavez has already warned all of us cowboys to stay clear of you. Hell, I don't blame him and he's right," Elliot said, leading Toter back to her stall.

"Listen to me, Elliot," she said angrily. "The man I am suppose to marry comes from a wealthy family in Mexico, but it was arranged and I had no say in the matter at that time. Now, I am a grown woman and I choose for myself whom I wish to marry. Do you understand?"

"Maria, I wish I could believe that but you are young, and ..."

"Young? Most women my age are already married and have children."

"Yes, but your father couldn't possibly understand any of this. He would think that I took advantage of you," he stammered, looking for a way out of this seemingly impossible situation.

"My father will understand, once I tell him."

"Tell him what?" Elliot said nervously.

She glared at him. "What does it take for me to get you to kiss me, Elliot?"

His eyes softened as he slowly lowered his head and kissed her full on the mouth, feeling her fingernails tug through his parka. As they pulled apart, the penetrating jasmine perfume fogged his brain. Her face was relaxed, but softly beautiful as he started to kiss her again.

"Elliot!" came a shout from the stable entrance.

Jerking around, he saw Chavez, frowning as he slowly walked toward them.

"How dare you disobey my order, senor. For this, you know what I must do." Chavez said.

"You will do nothing, Chavez," Maria said, scoldingly. "I will do as I please, when I please. I am no longer a child, and should I desire to have Elliot kiss me, then that is as it shall be. Is that clear, Chavez Ramon?"

Chavez, taken aback by this outburst, merely stammered, "But, senorita ..."

"Is that clear?"

"Yes, senorita, it is clear," he whispered, lowering his head.

Turning back to Elliot, she reached up, cupped his face in her hands, and kissed him quickly. Then, glancing at Chavez, she turned and hurried out of the stable.

Red-faced, Elliot looked at Chavez. "I'm sorry about this," he said, "I didn't want this to happen." It was a believable lie, Elliot thought.

Chavez looked at him and a slight smile lined his weathered face. "Do not be sorry, amigo. She is a grown woman and I always thought of her as a child. I am an old fool. But, as for you, I'm happy. I never did care for the Spanish family she was to marry into. They have a lot of pesos, to be sure, but weaklings, all of them. But her father must be informed of this."

"Well, I guess that'll be left up to me," Elliot said. "I'll tell him."

"Good," Chavez exclaimed. "It is something I don't wish to do, comprende?" Then he left, closing the door behind him.

I'll be damned, he mused. I'll just be damned.

Rafer came in at that moment leading his horse. "I just passed Chavez and he had a big grin on his face. What's going on?"

"He caught me and Maria kissing," Elliot said matter-of-factly.

"What? And he didn't shoot you?"

"No, fact is, he kind of liked it. But only after Maria gave him hell, partner."

"Well, I hope this means that at least I can keep my job," Rafer remarked.

"For now anyway."

"Huh?"

"Senor Paolo hasn't found out as yet."

"Oh hell, that's right. Anyway, it was just a kiss, wasn't it — nothing else?"

"I kind of think it might be a little more'n that, Rafe. Say, what's the deal with you and this Juanita?" he said, changing the subject.

"Yeah, ain't she something? I been seeing her off and on."

"Is it serious, partner?"

"It is with me and I think it is with her, too," Rafe said, grinning. "You won't hold it against me if I asked her to marry me, would you?"

"Hey, it was bound to happen, sooner or later, about us splitting up I mean. I hope that she will say yes."

"I think she will," Rafer said, putting up his horse. "I think she will."

"What's bothering you, Sonny?" Jenny inquired, watching as her husband absentmindedly twirled a drink.

Sonny looked up just as she sat down across from him at the table.

"You know that I talked to Frank Simpson about buying his place?"

"Uh-huh. So?"

"And he turned me down. He actually told me never to discuss it with him again," Sonny remarked. "Then I approached that greaser Paolo, and he turned me down, too."

"What the hell did you expect, Sonny? Paolo don't need your money. Besides, what do you want land for? We got everything we need right here. A ranch is nothing but hard work and headaches."

"Damn it, Jenny," Sonny said, "you just don't understand. I want to spread out. I feel cramped in this mangy town. I want respect. I want to be somebody. The Mex didn't work for his land. He had it handed to him. It ain't fair, having all that land, and me, nothing."

"If you're so all fired up to buy land, just go buy some somewhere else," she said irritably.

"Don't be silly, girl. Most of the land around here's only fit for rattlesnakes. He owns the best grazing area around."

"Then, do what you want," she blurted. "I don't care."

Sonny sat there for awhile after Jenny got up and retreated behind the bar. Then slowly he arose and started for the door. "Jenny, I'm going to El Paso. I'll be gone a couple of days."

"What, again?" she shouted. "What's so special in El Paso that you need to go there all the time? Maybe you might jump over to Juarez and get you a whore, huh?"

Ignoring that remark, he said, "Mind the store." Then he hurried out.

Elliot and Rafer were greasing a wheel to be put back on the wagon axle.

"When you gonna talk to Paolo about you and the senorita?" Rafer inquired.

"I think I'd better talk to her first before I do anything. It wasn't really brought up yesterday and, she's a woman, ain't she? Who knows what she's thinking today."

Looking up beyond Elliot, Rafer said, "Well, here's your chance. The senorita is coming."

"Good morning, gentlemen," Maria said, donning gloves. She was wearing brown tight riding breeches, tucked smartly in ankle boots. "Elliot, I'm going for a short ride. Would you join me?"

"Go ahead, partner," Rafer said. "I'll finish up this rig."

Elliot trotted Maria's pony out, saddled it, then handing her the reins, proceeded to saddle Toter.

Rafer watched them as they rode north.

After a brief spell riding, they reined up in the shadows of a cottonwood grove. They dismounted and she sat down as he tossed a few pebbles in a shallow stream.

"What are you thinking, Elliot?" she said.

He turned to her. "I need to know where we go from here, Maria. I mean just where do I stand?"

"Stand? What is that?" she said, teasingly.

"I mean we kissed and that was that or was it?"

She stood up and smiled. "Do you like my perfume, Elliot?" She came closer and he grabbed her, holding her at bay.

"Now dammit, girl, quit that. I want an answer."

"What is it that you want me to say?"

He stared at her momentarily feeling dejected. "Nothing. Nothing at all."

"Elliot, it was not just the kiss. Do you think that I'm in the habit of kissing men unless there was a feeling? I will say it. Yes, I do love you. I was in love with you the first day I saw you when you brought in the horses. Now, I have confessed. It is your turn."

Elliot could not fathom his good fortune. He quickly thought of Mary Louise and how glad he was now, not to have married her. He leaned down and kissed her.

"Well?" she said waiting.

"Maria, I ain't got much other than what I got on my back and Toter here, but I want to marry you."

"Was it so hard to say, my love?" she said, smiling. "Yes, I will marry you."

His heart leaped into his throat.

"Then," he stammered, "I need to talk to your father." He was so nervous, his voice was breaking.

"Yes, I believe that is the custom," she said, laughing. "Does it frighten you?"

He reached over and hugged her, then his eyes widened as he looked over her shoulder. Pulling away, he exclaimed, "Is that smoke over yonder?"

She turned around. "Yes, that must be near one of the line cabins, I think."

Leaping up, he grabbed his horse's reins.

"You get back to the ranch, Maria, and warn the others. I'm going to see what's happening."

"Elliot, please be careful," she shouted as he sped away.

He raced toward the billowing white smoke. It seemed to take forever to reach the burning structure, and then he noticed a dismounted figure, walking around. At first he felt alarm, but then he recognized Harry Two-Horse, and jumping down, raced over to him.

"Harry, what happened?"

Harry pointed to the ground. "Two riders have been here."

"Indians?" Elliot asked.

"No, not Indians, amigo. These horses were shod. Maybe Comancheros."

"Rustlers maybe?"

"It makes no sense for a rustler to burn an empty cabin, Elliot, if he was after cattle."

"Then, why would anyone want to set fire to an empty cabin?"

"Perhaps it is a warning of bad things to come, amigo," Harry said.

"What is that supposed to mean?"

"There are many that are jealous of the patron's ranchero. They wish to run us away, so they, like jackals, can take over this beautiful land. It is sad, but I have seen this coming for a long time. Come, let us go," Harry said, mounting.

They followed the arsonist's trail for awhile, then Harry stopped and knelt again, checking the ground.

"They do not care to cover their tracks," he said. "It is strange, or they are fools."

They remounted and continued.

Several Lazy P cowboys met them on the trail. Harry spoke to them in Spanish, explaining the event, then he sent them back to the ranch, as he felt he and Elliot could take care of matters. The two followed the fresh spoor which was heading west. Harry put his horse into a gallop, closing the gap.

After several miles, he again stopped, dismounted, and ran his hand gently on the tracks.

"They take their time, amigo," Harry said, looking up at Elliot. "Either they want us to catch up to them or. ... "

"Or what?" Elliot repeated.

"Or they are very stupid. Anyway, we must go with caution. There are many places here they could easily bushwhack us. Let us go."

A short time later, after crossing the Lazy P boundary, they came upon an Indian wickiup. There they found an elderly woman bending over a young brave. Harry conversed with her in Spanish while Elliot's horse pawed the ground anxiously. After a few words and gestures, little of which Elliot understood, Harry remounted and they moved away.

"They beat the young boy and took his woman with them. They are Comancheros," Harry said. "There is no hurry now, amigo."

"Why is that?" Elliot asked.

"They will stop before long to have their way with her, and when they tire of her, will either cut her throat or sell her. After all, my friend," he said, sarcastically, "she is Indian."

Night came after a short while, and they were about to stop when they saw a campfire glow in the distance.

"Could that be them?" Elliot asked.

"I cannot believe their stupidity," Harry said, dismounting. "From here, we walk."

Leading their ponies, they proceeded slowly toward the glow.

There were indeed only two of them, and one was already atop the woman as the other laughed and drank from a goatskin. The Indian woman did not scream nor fight her attacker.

"The one with his pants off is easy, the other we must take first," Harry whispered to Elliot. "He is mine. You go left and I go there." He pointed to the right. Elliot nodded and moved away.

The evening was briskly cold as Elliot tied his horse and advanced toward the trio, his rifle ready.

The men were laughing and completely oblivious of intruders. Harry was right, they were stupid. He and Harry had the distinct advantage, plus the fact they were sober, too.

Just as he positioned himself, a shot rang out and the comanchero with the bottle toppled backward.

Rising up, Elliot rushed forward. The half-naked comanchero jumped up off the squaw and bolted for his horse. Elliot shot at the man just as he leaped onto the horse's back. The slug caught him in the buttocks. He fell but reached up to grab the horse's reins. The horse, scared, reared and disappeared into the darkness, riderless.

Harry ran up to his victim, while Elliot rushed to his fallen quarry. Harry's target was dead. Elliot grabbed the wounded man, who was cursing him in Spanish, and dragged him closer to the fire.

The Indian woman had wrapped a blanket around her naked body and slowly walked toward them. When they met, she spat in the man's face, which was contorted in pain.

"We will take him back to the ranch," Harry said, "then he will tell us why they burned the cabin." He told the woman to put on her clothes and dress the man's wound to stop the bleeding. Later, they tied up the comanchero while putting more wood on the fire to ward off the chill.

Spreading his blanket down, Elliot moved as close to the fire as he could and finally drifted off to sleep. The sun was just peeking over the horizon when he heard a bone-chilling scream. Jumping up with his gun drawn, he witnessed the death throes of the comanchero as he rolled in the dust, blood spilling from his throat. The Indian woman stood over him, a bloody knife in her hand. Her face was emotionless. All Elliot could do was stare in horror. Finally, the jerking man lay still.

"Why the hell did she do that?" Elliot cried, looking at Harry.

Harry put his hand on him. "It is a matter of honor, amigo. I should have known this would happen. It is my fault. She was defiled by this man, disgraced, and probably will be beaten or cast away by her man."

"But now we'll never know if these hombres had been put up to this, will we?" Elliot remarked.

"I guess they were just passing through. No matter, perhaps in time we will know, my friend. The sun is up and it is time to go."

Saddling up, Elliot kept his eye on the Indian woman, who still hadn't uttered a word.

Harry gathered the dead men's belongings and draped them over the remaining horse. Handing the reins to the woman, he whispered a few words to her, and then mounted.

As they trotted away, Harry said, "She will take the horse and spoils back to her wickiup and her man will have the choice of accepting it, or keep it and run her off. But, I believe that the horse will help. Either way, it is done."

"She is a cold one, all right," Elliot said. "She didn't blink an eye when she slit his throat."

"It is not uncommon, amigo. The Indian has little to say, but emotions run very deep. Besides, it is a hard country, and life is short, too short."

Harry related the event in the presence of Paolo and Chavez, as Elliot looked on. Chavez said that it was too late to rebuild the destroyed cabin and that whoever was in the nearest cabin would have to pull double duty.

Paolo turned to Elliot then and said, "Again, Elliot, we are indebted to you."

"It's part of my job, senor," he replied.

'It is not my wish that you become a pistolero, my friend," Paolo said, shaking his head. "It is not good. If only we could be left in peace."

The meeting broke up and they headed for the door. Elliot, suddenly seized by a thought, turned and looked at Paolo.

"Sir, could I talk to you in private?" Chavez grinned at him as he passed. "Certainly, my boy," Paolo said, lighting up a cigar. "Sir," Elliot began, taking out his neckerchief and wiping his brow. "Well, what is it you wish to speak to me about?" "Senor, it is about the senorita." "Do you mean Maria?" questioned Paolo.

Elliot nodded nervously. "Yes sir, we've been seeing one another." "You have been with my daughter?" Paolo said, surprised. He stamped out his cigar. "Yes sir, and we want to get married. I know that..."

"One moment, Elliot," Paolo interrupted. He went to the door and opened it, only to find that Maria was standing there sheepishly.

"Maria Evita, my child, please do come in," Paolo said, "and explain yourself."

She walked in, and without looking at Elliot, sat down.

"Is this true?" Paolo asked. "You have been seeing Senor Elliot?"

"Yes, father," she retorted, glancing in Elliot's direction.

At this remark, Paolo clasped his hands behind his back, went to the window and gazed out.

"Father, he wishes to marry me, and I desire it too."

"And where was Consuelo all this time?" Paolo blurted, turning to her.

"Do not blame Consuelo, father. She knew nothing of this," Maria said.

"Senor Elliot, you must understand. You had no right. As you were no doubt told, she is betrothed to another man."

"Yessir, I know that."

"Maria, you know that if you persist in this, that I must inform the Aragons. I will be embarrassed and they will be insulted," Paolo said. "Your poor mother looked with favor on the arrangement. Do you remember?"

"Yes, father, and I am sorry," Maria said, "but this is my choice, as before I had none."

Paolo reached for a fresh cigar and lit it as he paced around the room.

Maria looked up at Elliot and smiled weakly.

Elliot shifted around becoming nervous while waiting for Paolo's next move.

Standing and looking out of the window, Paolo took his time. Sweat broke out on Elliot's forehead.

Paolo finally turned and looked directly at Elliot. "I must have time to think on this."

"But, father ..." Maria cried.

"Hush, my child. You are very young and impressionable. Perhaps you truly love one another, but I have a custom and honor I must follow. I hope, senor Elliot, that you understand. You are a fine young man. Now, please, I would like to be alone."

Maria, with tears in her eyes, fled the room.

Elliot, hesitatingly, started to speak but felt better of it. He then left.

Outside, Chavez was waiting, but upon looking at Elliot's expression, knew the outcome.

"I'm sorry, Elliot," he said, to a silently retreating Elliot.

That evening, he laid in his bunk and cursed his luck. He didn't blame Paolo. After all, Paolo was hoping Maria would marry a Mexican gentleman who had a better upbringing than he. Paolo wanted a son-in-law who could speak his own language and observe their traditions.

He should never had gotten involved with Maria — beautiful Maria. If he can't have her then he couldn't stay on the ranch and have to gaze upon her every day. This, he was sure of. Well, he thought, we'll see. Sleep was difficult that night.

Elliot did not see Maria for the next two days outside of the main house. It was just as well.

Things were slow around the ranch and Chavez gave everyone a free day from work.

Elliot, Billy and Rafer rode into Las Cruces and went straight to Mason's bar. Elliot saw Jenny but chose to ignore her as the three ordered whiskey. That evening the trio were thoroughly drunk when deputy Trent came in.

"Why, hello there deputy," Billy shouted. "Can I buy you a drink?"

"No, thank you. Are you fellows celebrating something?" Trent asked.

"Yep," Billy said. "We're celebrating a much-needed day of rest. Ain't that right, boys?"

"Well, you fellas have fun but keep it down a little, will you?" Then Trent left.

They did not notice Rusty Murtaugh who came in passing Trent. Rusty went to the bar and ordered a drink.

Jenny behind the bar, sauntered over.

"Any one of them boys over there go by the name of Stewart?" Rusty asked.

"Yeah," Jenny replied, "the tall good looking one. Why you asking?"

"He killed my brother, Jenny and I aim to make him pay."

"I knew your brother was dead but I didn't know it was Elliot there that killed him. Well, would you believe. They are pretty drunk and I'm sure you can take him easy, Rusty."

"Maybe. Maybe yes, maybe no. There ain't no hurry, miz Jenny. In my own good time, he will pay."

"Here," Jenny said, "have another drink on the house."

"Why are you giving me a free drink, anyway?"

"Let's just say that I ain't got no love lost on that hombre, either," Jenny whispered, pouring his tumbler full. He downed it in one gulp, winked at her and left.

"Hell, Elliot, let's us go on down to that there whorehouse and get us some girls. What do you say?" Rafer said.

"Yeah, that's a damned good idea," Billy replied. "C'mon, Elliot, you'll enjoy it."

"I don't know, boys. I've had too much to drink," Elliot said, sheepishly.

"Aw, c'mon, Elliot," Rafer said. "It will do you good." He pulled on Elliot who, slowly got up.

The night was cold as they trudged towards the two-story house. Entering, they confronted the madam.

"Give us three of your best," Billy demanded, pulling bills out of his jeans.

Elliot followed the girl to an upstairs room. She began to take off her clothes but as she started for the bed, stopped, as Elliot's snoring told her it was useless to continue. She covered him with a sheet and laid down beside him. Oh well, she thought, she had made her money for the evening.

Later, Billy, who was sleeping in a room directly below Elliot's, woke up, A creaking outside alerted him. Then a shadow crossed the window. He glanced at the sleeping girl, then turned out of the bed, reached for his holster and got his gun. His brain was foggy, but he did not like creeping shadows in the night. Slowly, he went to the window, pulled apart the curtains and saw the shadow above him. He stepped out onto the ground and looked up.

The sinister figure slowly opened the window, aimed and pulled the trigger.

Elliot jumped up as the blast was deafening.

"Hold it right there," Billy shouted.

The man turned and shot wildly at Billy who ducked, but answered with a slug. The ambusher jumped from the landing, somersaulted once and came up running.

Looking out the window with a cocked six-shooter, Elliot shouted, "What's going on?"

"Somebody shot into your window, Elliot," Billy shouted. "Are you hurt?"

"No, but who was it?"

"I don't know. I guess I missed him, though. He's gone."

Elliot turned and fumbling in his pocket, found a match and lit the wall gas lamp. As the light bathed the room he saw, with horror, a young woman, lying in his bed, dead.

A few moments later, deputy Trent rushed in, along with the madam and Billy.

"What happened?" Trent asked.

"Some drygulcher shot into Elliot's bedroom, deputy. I shot at him but I guess I missed. I drank too much tonight, otherwise I would've got him. Damn it anyway," Billy cursed. "He was a big man. That's all I can tell you."

"I got to get out of here," Elliot said. "I'm going to be sick."

"Easy, partner," Billy said, quietly, "easy."

"No, I mean it. Let's get out of this town. Where's Rafe?"

Directed by the madam, they went in and woke Rafer. He had slept through the affair and was reluctant to leave, trying to turn over and resume his stupor. They finally got him dressed and mounting their horses, departed Las Cruces. Out on the plains they stopped for the remainder of the night.

Sitting around a small fire, they huddled close.

"I traded a nice warm bed for this?" Rafer said, quivering in his parka.

"You think it might have been that Murtaugh that tried to do you in?" Billy said.

"Who else could it have been?" Elliot replied. "I figure he's no better than his brother. You know, you try to keep away from trouble and the more you get into it,"

"Yeah," Rafe interjected. "You know that this ain't the end of Murtaugh. Sooner or later, Elliot, you're gonna have to deal with that back-shooter."

"So, how was your girl last night, Elliot. Did you enjoy her?" Billy asked.

"Huh? Hell Billy, I was so drunk I don't remember even going to bed, much less doing anything with that girl."

"You mean we paid good money for her and you didn't even have her?"

"I guess not."

"Damn, Elliot," Rafer said, laughing. "You lost all the way around, didn't you?"

"I reckon so," Elliot said. "Oh, before I forget, fellas. Don't let on back at the ranch about that woman. If Maria finds out, I'm dead meat for sure."

Billy and Rafer laughed aloud.

11

It was afternoon when Sonny Mason strode into the El Paso saloon.

"Hey, Sonny, what're you doing in town?" the proprietor said.

"Hello, Mooney, gimme a drink, will you?"

Downing the drink rapidly, Sonny ordered another. Looking around, he was disappointed. There were very few patrons in the saloon.

"Yeah, things have been pretty slow around here," Mooney said. "The soldiers don't get paid for another three days."

"Mooney, you know where I can hire a gunman?"

"What's the matter? You got trouble, Sonny?"

"No, not yet anyway. Well, do you?" Sonny inquired.

"Well, I know for sure that Bodine's in town," the owner said emphatically.

"Bodine? You mean Pete Bodine from up Roswell way?"

"Yep, and I believe he's in the hotel right now," Mooney said, wiping the bar. "He's got the sheriff as nervous as a cat in heat. If you can get him out of town, the sheriff would be beholden to you. That's for sure."

"Thanks," Sonny said, quickly finishing his drink. "I owe you one."

The hostelry was across the street, and Sonny impatiently inquired as to Bodine's room number, then bounded up the stairs.

A knock on the door alerted the occupant, and Sonny heard the shuffling of feet.

"Who's there?"

"Bodine? My name is Sonny Mason from Las Cruces, and I have a proposition for you. Are you interested?"

Cautiously unlocking the door, Bodine stepped back as Sonny entered. Bodine had a cocked pistol in his hand. Noticing Sonny was unarmed, he holstered it.

"So, Mr. Mason, what's your proposition?"

Sonny quickly measured the gunman. Bodine was small in stature, which belied his reputation. His hair was dark and slicked down, and a razor thin mustache graced his upper lip.

Bodine sat on the edge of the bed and pulled on his boots. "Well?" he said, looking up, and it was then that Sonny noticed the pale, piercing blue eyes.

"I have a job for you, Bodine."

"You do, eh? What kind of job are you referring to?"

"I've got my eye on a ranch and the owner refuses to sell. . ."

"So, you want me to help you get it, huh?" Bodine finished. He pulled out a small cigar and lit it up. "Where's this ranch?"

"It's near Las Cruces," Sonny said, "called the Lazy P."

Bodine whistled and stared at him. "The Lazy P, you say? Man, you aim big, don't you? If I take the job, it will cost you quite a bit."

"I'll pay what's reasonable," Sonny replied. "How many men you got?"

"None at the moment, Mason. I can get four, maybe five," Bodine said, glancing out the window. "Are there any gunslingers on that ranch?"

"Naw, just some Mexican cowhands. There ain't nobody worth mentioning that's good with an iron."

"And where do I find you when I get there?" Bodine asked.

"Everybody knows where Sonny Mason's Bar is in Las Cruces. Just ask. So, you will take the job then?"

"I'll think about it. If I can round up enough men, we should be there in a few days. Anything else?"

"I guess that's it," Sonny said and savoring an unexpected feeling of satisfaction, left.

"What's the matter with the shooters in this damned place anyway?" Jenny inquired, sipping at the bar with Murtaugh. "You had him dead to rights and you messed it up."

"Well, it was dark and I really couldn't see all that good, Jenny. But there'll be another time. I ain't done yet," Rusty replied. "Where's Sonny anyway?"

"Hell, he's down in El Paso, probably humping some greaser gal in Juarez. He never tells me what he's doing, anyhow." She downed another shot. "Damn that Stewart."

"So why do you have it in for this Stewart, Jenny?"

She looked at him hard. "He's so high and mighty coming to town like he owned it and insulting me."

"So, why'd you not go to the sheriff about it?" he asked.

"Gentry? Gentry ain't gonna do nothing for me or Sonny. He's got no use for us. And Sonny ain't gonna do nothing at all. I got to do everything myself, seems like."

"Now, don't you worry about it. I got it in for this Stewart, and he's gonna die."

"Rusty, you and your brother never did like each other; so why are you so dead set on getting Stewart?"

"I can't allow nobody to gun down a Murtaugh. Naw, I wasn't crazy about Jim, but he's kin."

"Here, take another drink," Jenny said, pouring, "and get out of here." She turned away.

"Chavez," Paolo called, "will you be going to town soon?"

"Si, patron, today in fact. We need more supplies. Is there something you wish for me to get?"

"No, but I want you to take this message to the telegraph office and send it. You are to tell no one of it. Comprende?"

"Si, patron," Chavez replied, pocketing the message and turned. "Jose, get the buckboard ready. We must go to Las Cruces."

Jose hurried to the corral for a pair of horses to hitch to the buckboard.

"Elliot," Chavez yelled. "I want you to accompany us." He did not see Maria, who heard him.

"Chavez, I wish to go along. I want to buy some cloth. I will tell father."

In a few moments, Maria came out followed by Consuelo. The two took their places on the rear wagon seat as Jose slapped the reins.

Chavez was in the front as Elliot rode drag. On occasion, Maria would turn to look at him, and he would touch the brim of his hat and smile.

As the entourage drove down the street of Las Cruces, Elliot spied Jenny Mason in front of her saloon, her arms folded under her breasts. He felt she had a smirk on her face rather than a smile. As they passed her, she turned and re-entered the saloon. Reining up in front of the general store and warehouse, the men went in as Maria and Consuelo walked to the dress goods emporium to browse.

Elliot and Jose lugged purchases and stacked them in the buck-board and returned for more. When the buckboard was near capacity, Elliot, needing some cartridges, stepped into another store while Jose climbed up on the wagon seat and waited.

Chavez walked over to the telegraph office and handed the operator the message. The operator read it out loud then asked Chavez for payment. Chavez turned to leave and knowing the contents of the wire, shook his head.

Elliot emerged with several boxes of ammunition when he noticed the expression on Jose's face. He turned and saw two men in front of Maria and Consuelo, blocking their path.

Tossing the boxes into the buckboard, he hurried toward the group, unloosing his hammer tie-down.

"You're a mighty pretty thing, for a Mex," one said, grinning. "How's about we go over yonder to the saloon and I'll buy you a drink. Your girlfriend there can be with my partner."

"Senor," Maria said, "you are insulting. Now let us pass, undalay pronto."

Elliot reached them just as the man grabbed Maria's arm. She struck him hard across the face and Elliot grabbed him, spun him around, then hit him full in the nose. The man fell backward as Consuelo screamed. The other went for his gun, but just as he touched his weapon, Elliot's gun had cleared, the hammer cocked.

"Don't do nothing foolish, mister," Elliot said with a snarl, "or you're a dead man."

The man's eyeballs widened at this display of quickness.

'Hey," called a voice behind them.

Elliot dropped down and spun around.

"Hold it, son. It's me, Sheriff Gentry."

He lowered, then sheathed his pistol.

"Stewart, ain't it? I saw it all and I'll take over from here," the sheriff said. Turning to the two men, he snarled. "You two go on back to Jenny and tell her it didn't work."

Surprised, Elliot said, "Jenny?"

"Yeah," the sheriff replied. "I was watching everything. These two hard noses came out of Mason's and made a beeline for your women here, but I figured they was really after you."

Elliot glanced toward the saloon and glimpsed Jenny ducking away from the entrance. My lord, he thought, she certainly carries a lasting grudge, and over nothing. He escorted the women back to the buckboard.

As they got aboard, Elliot angrily told Jose to move on out of town and that he would catch up to them. Then he hurried off to the saloon and with each step, enragement built up. At the saloon entrance, he paused and glanced back, seeing the puzzled look on Maria's face. His face expressionless, he turned and entered.

Unknowing to the buckboard passengers, Rusty Murtaugh had witnessed the incident and stepping closer, he remarked. "That man there was caught sleeping the other night with one of them whores down the street. Maybe, he's been bedding down Miz Jenny, too, and she don't like it. Tsk, tsk."

Maria's face turned livid.

"Go from here, gringo," Consuelo shouted.

"She's right," Chavez said, looking hard at Rusty. "You had best move on."

Smiling, Murtaugh tipped his hat and backed away.

"Want a drink, Elliot?" Jenny said, smirking.

"Naw, Jenny, but I came to warn you. You get off my case. I

don't play games and because of your actions, people are getting hurt and killed. Just leave me alone. Can you understand plain English?"

"Elliot, you can just go to hell," she said angrily and turned her back to him.

"Just remember what I said, Jenny," he remarked. "Don't give me no reason to come back. If I do come back, the first thing I'm going to do is tell your husband the truth. Then we'll see what happens. Either way you're gonna lose."

He turned and walked out. Mounting Toter, he rode after the buckboard.

Back at the ranch, Maria took him aside and demanded an explanation. He told her of the night Jenny invaded his bedroom but swore nothing came of it.

"And what of the other woman?" she demanded angrily.

Taken aback, he stammered, "What other woman?"

'The whore that you did sleep with."

"Hell, Maria, I was drunk, besides, she was killed that night," he said.

"Elliot, maybe my father was correct in having second thoughts about our marriage. Now, I certainly do!" She spun around and hurriedly left.

"But, Maria..." he called, but she was gone. Staring after her, he felt his world had caved in on him. He took off his hat and slammed it to the ground.

"Easy, partner, easy," Rafer said, trying to soothe him.

Elliot had not noticed him approaching.

"Dammit, Rafe, you try to do the best you can and this happens," Elliot said disgusted.

"I know, man. You can't figure women."

"I've lost her for sure."

"No you ain't lost her. If she really cares for you, she'll stew for awhile and then she'll come around. You'll see."

"I don't know, Rafe," he said shaking his head. "I just don't know. If I can't get her back, I ain't staying. I can't stay. Do you understand?"

"C'mon, let's go to the bunkhouse and get ready for supper. I'm starving," Rafer declared.

As they crossed the area, Elliot slowed momentarily and gazed into the corral.

"You really have an eye for that black one yonder, don't you, partner," Rafer remarked.

"Yeah, he's a beauty all right."

"Hell, even if you wanted to own him, you couldn't afford him, Elliot. Besides, I don't think that Paolo will ever sell him. He's stud material."

"You're right."

They continued towards the bunkhouse.

12

November brought cooler weather and gusty winds. The days began to shorten as the ranch hands gathered and stored hay for the animals. The Arabian horses, not used to this extreme cold, were placed in various stables to get them out of the wind.

Late one afternoon, riders approached the ranch, led by Sheriff Tom Gentry. Paolo hailed them and Elliot noticed it was a somber group of townsmen.

"Senor, I have bad news," Tom said. "Frank Simpson's been killed, and his wife and daughter have been kidnaped by renegades. Several of his hands have been injured, and his cook's dead, also."

"Madre mia," Paolo shouted, stunned at the news, "who would do such a thing?"

"We don't know. I got together a posse, but these men here ain't that good with guns, so I come to ask you for a few of your men."

Gathering closer, the cowhands looked to Paolo.

"Of course, sheriff, take whoever you require. Frank Simpson was a good, hard working Christian man. He did not deserve this," Paolo lamented. Turning to his cowhands, he said, shakily, "Who wishes to go with the sheriff?"

All pressed forward, raising their hands. Paolo nodded, seemingly impressed and proud of this gesture.

'Thanks, fellas, but I don't need all of you," Tom said. "Just a couple of good gun hands, but I would like Harry Two-Horse to go."

"Yes, take Harry, by all means," Paolo said.

"I want to go," Billy said. Elliot and Rafer stepped forward, also.

"That's good," Tom said, "I was hoping I could count on you, Elliot. Get your mounts and your guns. We got enough grub with us, but take your bedrolls and warm clothing. We may be gone a few days."

Each went their way to saddle up.

Maria came out of the house and asked Chavez what was going on. When he told her, she was stunned. "What of Carol?"

"I do not know, child, but I dread the worst."

She placed her hand on his arm and he looked down at her.

"You will bring Elliot back, safe," she said.

He smiled at her and nodded. Then he mounted and joined the others.

The posse, now numbering ten, sped toward the Simpson ranch. When they arrived, Elliot was appalled at the devastation. The family home was burned to the ground, as was the bunkhouse and barn. The corral gate was broken and all the animals had scattered.

A cowboy with a bloody bandage around his thigh limped toward them.

"Talk to me, amigo," Tom said, "and fast!"

"Bandits, sheriff, many banditos," the cowboy exclaimed, in pain.

"How many?"

"I'm not sure, maybe eight, maybe nine," he said, gripping his leg. "They take the senora and the child with them. They are Mexicanos."

"Compadre," Harry said, "bury your dead. Take everyone and go to the Lazy P ranch. They will take care of you."

"Gracias, amigo," the cowhand said, taking off his hat.

"Let's go men," Tom shouted. "Harry, you take the lead." The group turned and headed out.

Harry was having no trouble following the trail. After a few miles, he stopped the posse and dismounted, asking the sheriff and Elliot to join him.

"As you can see, Tom, they are heading for Mexico along the trail to Palomos," Harry said, pointing.

"Yes, I can see that."

"They are about four hours ahead of us, and they must know we are following them."

"So far, it makes sense. Go on."

Harry gazed into the distance. "It is not good to follow too closely. They will kill the women if they see us. It would be better to get ahead of them, and the only place for them to turn south would be at Jimano Pass, then it would be straight to the border. But, in order to get ahead of them, we must ride all night, Tom."

"I like that better," Tom said, looking back at his men. "They most likely won't be looking in front of them. Let's do it." He informed the posse members of his decision.

As the group headed off, Elliot knew that if the kidnappers stopped for any length of time, they would abuse the women, maybe kill them. His blood chilled at the thought. During the grueling trek, the men ate on the move. Parched corn and jerky was all that they'd brought. When the horses tired, they dismounted and walked them for thirty minutes, then remounted and continued. Rafer complained often of his sore buttocks.

Catching up to Harry, Elliot said, "You know this country well?"

"Yes, amigo. Many years ago, my father's wickiup was just a few miles west of here. I used to play in these hills and I know it well."

"How'd you happen to join up with Senor Paolo?" Elliot asked.

"I was very young when my parents died. I was an only child and Chavez found me and took me to the ranch. There I have been and I will lay down my life for Chavez or the patron, amigo."

"I have heard that before, Harry," Elliot said.

"It is my hope that these renegades will stop for a while. They may think that they are not being followed too closely and relax their guard."

"Yes, but if they stop," Elliot remarked, "they may hurt the women."

"That's true enough, but we have no choice," Harry said, shrugging his shoulders. "The women may be dead already. I don't think so, unless they put up a fight."

The night was cold and once again, they dismounted to walk the horses. Rafer's limp was more pronounced by this time, and Elliot knew his partner was in pain. One of the townsmen informed the sheriff that his horse had gone lame. Tom told him to camp for the night and return to Las Cruces the next day.

"Well, Devon," Sonny whispered, pouring him a drink, "you did a good job." "Sonny, I ain't proud of what I did, but I needed the money," Devon said, hoisting and gulping the shot glass. "Gimme another."

"You didn't have no trouble finding that bunch of renegades, did you?"

"No, but they didn't have to kill Simpson and take the women. Do you know what they're gonna do with them girls? It ain't gonna be pretty."

"They got paid well. Simpson had no call to talk to me the way he did, so I ain't gonna lose no sleep over it. Besides, when Bodine gets here, you can join up with him, that'll mean more money in your poke."

"Yeah, once I get enough money, I'm leaving these parts and go on to California."

Sonny looked up and stiffened. "Oh-oh, here comes Jenny. Don't say nothing."

By morning, the pace had slowed considerably because both men and horses were exhausted. Elliot saw Harry raise his hand.

"There, about four miles ahead, is the border," Harry said. "They have not come this way, so we are ahead of them, amigos."

"Good," Tom declared. Then he called his men to gather around him. "Boys, they will be coming from that direction, and we got between them and the border. So check your weapons and take positions behind any cover you can find. And, above all, watch for the women. We don't want them hurt. Choose a man and drop him with your first shot. The quicker we drop them all, the safer the women will be. Mark, you take all the horses and head for that stream bed yonder and stay with them, you hear? Okay, any questions?"

One of the townsmen spoke up. "You mean we're going to dry gulch them, Tom?"

Elliot, thinking it a dumb question, had to bite his tongue, but the sheriff lashed out for him.

"Look, I ain't got time to worry about them. I got to worry about us and them women, you understand me?" Tom said. "Now scatter and take up your positions. I'll fire the first shot. Let's move!"

Elliot grabbed his rifle and went to hide behind a group of sage-brushes. Rafer was to his right and Billy slightly in front. He thought it amusing that Billy would try to get ahead of everyone and knew he wouldn't wait for the sheriff to take the first shot. Although it was cool, he felt sweat trickle down his forehead. His body cried for rest and sleep.

About an hour had passed when Elliot, stiff and almost groggy, discerned riders to the north. A dust cloud swirled upward and then disintegrated. As the riders drew closer, he counted nine men and one woman alone on a pony. He strained to find the second woman, but she wasn't with them. He recognized the daughter, but where was her mother?

He saw Billy slowly raise his rifle. Elliot also took careful aim as he watched the renegades casually riding into their ambush.

Suddenly, Billy's rifle shattered the stillness. Then it seemed that the world exploded in gunfire. Elliot shot at his man, but it appeared no less than three balls hit him simultaneously as he tumbled backward. Rising up, Billy drew his pistol and rushed forward, firing at others. Damn, thought Elliot, that kid's got nerve.

Riderless horses scattered in all directions, raising clouds of dust. Elliot raised up to see through the dust, but there was so much confusion, he couldn't find a target. Several bullets zinged past him, but they seemed to be from posse members indiscriminately firing as they pushed forward, too.

In a matter of seconds, it was all over. Elliot then slowly walked among the bodies. Five of the Mexicans had been killed instantly and three were wounded, one badly. Only one of the renegades was unscathed, his hands were raised in surrender.

Sheriff Gentry rushed to the girl's pony and grabbed the reins of the wild-eyed creature. The girl toppled into Rafer's arms, crying uncontrollably.

"We got you, honey," he said. "You're all right now."

Her face was dirty and her clothes torn. She was barefoot and bleeding.

"They killed my mother," she cried, her body shaking. "They killed my mother."

"The bastards!" Billy shouted. "The dirty, stinking bastards."

Sheriff Gentry tried to console the child. She seemed utterly exhausted and finally drifted into quiet sobs. Rafer stood up with tears in his eyes. He looked at one of the gut-shot Mexicans who was moaning in Spanish.

"What's he saying?" he asked, looking at Harry.

"He begs you to shoot him and put him out of his misery," Harry said, spitting on the man.

"I got no problem with that," Billy said, and coolly shot him between the eyes.

Two of the posse members approached Tom, who was still holding the girl.

"Sheriff, what do we do with these hombres?" one said.

"Hell, I don't care," Tom said, looking up at them. "This ain't in my jurisdiction. Do what you want with them."

Billy, rifling through the bandit's belongings, held up a saddle bag. "Look, men, this bag's full of greenbacks and gold coins too."

"I guess that's Simpson's money, more'n likely," Elliot said, checking the saddle on his pony.

"We better take all this back with us," Billy remarked. "That girl there is going to need it."

A shot rang out and Elliot turned. Then another shot rang out. He saw that the riders were methodically executing the wounded bandits. When it was over, they calmly stepped over the dead and many spat on them.

As the group gathered to leave, the sheriff mounted, and the sobbing girl was handed to him. He held her close and said, "Boys, let's backtrack and find Mrs. Simpson and give her a proper burial."

About five miles north, they found the former campsite and Mrs. Simpson, who lay in a crumpled heap off to the side. The daughter started crying anew as they solemnly buried her mother. Elliot clenched his teeth as he tried to hold back tears. What a waste, he thought. What a terrible waste.

As they started on the trail homeward, Billy muttered something inaudible.

"What's that, Billy?" he said.

"I said, nothing but a bunch of animals would do a thing like that."

"Yeah, animals."

When the tired group reached the Lazy P, Paolo and the others were waiting for them.

Simpson's daughter was bound over to Maria, who, with Consuelo, quickly took her into the house. Then Tom related the incident to Paolo, who shook his head throughout.

"It is such a shame," Paolo said. "The Simpson's were good people. We will take care of the child and the ranch. Gracias, Tom, and to all of you for what you have done."

"You should thank Harry Two-Horse for this. We didn't lose a man thanks to him," Tom said. "He's the best tracker I know."

Harry bowed his head appreciatively.

Turning to the borrowed posse members, Tom thanked them for their help, then he and the townsmen departed.

Chavez told his men to rest for the remainder of the day. Elliot collapsed in his bunk and immediately went to sleep.

Rafer groaned as he, too, laid down.

Chavez, unsaddling his horse, was confronted by Maria. "It went well, senorita. Elliot did good. Is that what you meant to ask?"

"Yes," she said.

"Senorita?"

"What is it?"

"Nothing - nothing, my child," he said and turned away. He had made a promise.

It took several days to calm the young Carol down, although everyone whispered that she would be scarred for life. In an effort to soothe things for Carol, Maria took her first to Las Cruces, and then to El Paso to purchase some new apparel. It was decided that Carol would become part of the Paolo family until she became a woman.

Elliot felt that Maria was avoiding him and his self-esteem was low, so he worked as hard as he could to get his mind off her.

He had noticed that Rafer was squiring Juanita around quite often. Any free time Rafer could find was spent with her. Elliot was pleased that Rafer had, at long last, found a woman he could be close to.

13

onny watched from the doorway of his office as Pete Bodine and five other hard cases walked into the bar. Seating themselves at two tables, they waited for the bartender.

"Yessir, gents, what'll it be?" he asked.

"Tell Mason I want to see him" Bodine said, looking the premises over.

At that time, Sonny emerged and hurried over, holding out his hand. "Bodine, it's good to see you." Then noticing Deputy Trent peering into the bar, he hustled Pete toward his office, pausing only to tell the rest to order drinks on the house.

As he entered the office, Sonny ordered Jenny to get out. Looking Pete up and down, she left without a word.

"I saw the sheriffs deputy looking in, so the sheriff will know soon enough that you're here," Sonny said. "We need to get our business done and you leave town." He quickly, but thoroughly informed Bodine about the Lazy P and how many hands were there.

"Now you told me there wasn't no gunners at the Lazy P, right?" Bodine said, pouring himself a drink.

"Nothing to speak of. There's a kid up there by the name of Billy that's pretty fair, so I hear, and a drifter named Elliot Stewart. But the ones to watch are Chavez Ramon, the ramrod, and an Indian, Harry Two-Horse. Harry can be mean, excellent with a knife, so-so with a handgun."

"Okay, so how do you want me to work this? I'm not about to go rushing in and . . ."

"No," Sonny said, "I got a plan. Before long, the hands will pair up and go to several line cabins for the winter. There won't be five hands left at the house. I have drawn a map that shows about where the cabins are found, and with your men, you can isolate them and take them one by one. Get rid of the wranglers, but don't burn the cabins. A fire can be seen for miles. Besides, when I take over I don't need to spend extra money building new cabins. If you do a quick job, you can get rid of most of them before the word spreads."

"You got it all figured out, don't you?" Bodine said. "But just getting rid of the wranglers ain't gonna necessarily get you the ranch."

"With them out of the way, I can force Paolo to come to terms," Sonny said, lighting a cigar.

"And if he don't?"

"I'll worry about that later. Who knows, maybe we can get rid of him, too. Then that just leaves the girl," Sonny said, grinning.

"The girl?"

"His young daughter. She's pretty, but she can't run that large spread by herself. So, if I can get the Lazy P, then old Frank Simpson's place will be up for grabs, too."

"Yeah," Bodine said, sipping his drink. "I heard about that. Now, I got gunners I need to take care of. What kind of pay you offering?"

"I'll pay each of your boys two hundred dollars, and you get one thousand. How's that?"

"Ain't good enough, Mason. This is gonna be a big job. My boys get five hundred apiece, and I get two thousand, or we go our way."

Frowning, Sonny stood up and paced the floor.

"Damn, that's a lot of money, Bodine."

"That's my price. Take it or leave it."

"Okay, okay, agreed," Sonny said.

"Where do we stay until you need us?" Bodine said, rising. "If we stay in town, the sheriff is going to start nosing around and I don't like it."

"Oh yeah, I got a two-story house near a town called Deming, west of here. It's empty, so you fellas can stay there until I get word to you. It's already stocked with provisions and plenty of whiskey.

"Good," Bodine said, and he smiled deviously.

As they walked out of the office, Jenny was lurking near the door, obviously eavesdropping. Sonny glared at her, but Bodine just glanced her way and motioned his bunch to follow him out. Sonny accompanied him to his horse as Sheriff Gentry walked up.

Seeing his badge, Bodine, held the reins of his pinto. "Can we help you, sheriff?"

"You're Pete Bodine, ain't you," Tom said. "I need to know if you and your friends here are just passing through." His gaze took in the hard-looking bunch in one sweep.

"We're just passing through, sheriff," Bodine said, "and as you can see, we're leaving now. Any problem with that?" He grinned, mounted his pinto then he and the others rode away.

Tom looked hard at Sonny as he returned to his saloon. Going to the bar, he told the bartender to pour him a drink and sat down on a stool.

"Sonny, come over here," a familiar voice demanded.

Turning around, Sonny saw Rusty Murtaugh at a table in the corner. Sonny waited for his drink then casually walked over.

"Sit down a minute," Rusty said. "What's going on?"

Sonny flinched. "Nothing, why?"

"I heard the Lazy P mentioned, and there's a cowhand there that I want. He killed my brother."

"Your brother, eh? Who was supposed to have killed your brother?"

"A man by the name of Elliot Stewart. Do you know him?"

"I heard of him, Rusty. Okay, you stick around and maybe we can help each other," Sonny said. He got up to leave, but Rusty grabbed him, his huge hands were painfully clamped on Sonny's arm.

"I ain't gonna wait long," Rusty said, staring at him.

When he was finally released by the big man, Sonny went into his office. Jenny was sitting at his desk, thumping her fingers and glaring at him.

"What's your problem?" Sonny asked, heading for the safe.

"You're bound and determined to get that ranch, ain't you?" Jenny remarked.

"Yeah, I want it bad. So?"

"Damn it, Sonny, with Simpson dead, you could have his place without any killing. Why mess with Paolo's bunch? It ain't like them to roll over and play possum. You know Gentry's crazy about the Lazy P outfit, and he ain't gonna sit by and watch you kill them off."

"Jenny, let me be. I know what I'm doing. If I got it planned right, we can have not only the Lazy P, but Simpson's as well. You could be queen of over twenty thousand acres. Think about it a minute. I'm saying twenty thousand, honey," Sonny said, opening the safe. He began counting bills.

"You better hope it don't backfire on you," Jenny said, getting up and settling down on the couch. He didn't reply. Satisfied that he had sufficient money on hand, he got up and left the office.

Elliot was working in one of the stables when he thought he heard horses moving outside. Looking out the door, he was surprised to see about fifteen mounted soldiers riding toward the house. This was the first time he had seen soldiers other than at Fort Bliss. Curious, he began walking behind them.

The soldiers pulled up in front of the house just as Paolo emerged. Greeting them, he inquired of the lieutenant the reason for them being so far north

"A few weeks back, a gang of bandits shot up the village of Serpentine in Texas and came this way. We lost track of them about twenty miles back, senor," the lieutenant said.

"Ah, they must be the same banditos that raided and burned the Simpson ranch, officer, north of here," Paolo said, pointing. "His daughter now lives with us here as her father and mother were killed."

"I'm sorry to hear that, senor," the officer exclaimed. "I only wish we could have gotten here sooner."

"I think that they are all dead now, as a posse rode them down, officer." Paolo said. "Well, that's good to hear," the lieutenant said as he turned in the saddle to look over the ranch. Elliot saw his head jerk as he spotted the thoroughbreds.

"Them's some fine looking horses you got there. Can't say as I've ever seen that kind before, sir."

"Come, I show you, my son," Paolo said, beaming, as he led the way.

Elliot followed the troop as they retreated to the corral.

"Just what do you intend to do with that breed, sir?" the lieutenant inquired.

"I intend to breed them to the quarter horses and hope to have a superior animal."

The lieutenant leaned forward in his saddle. "How much will you take for that black stallion, sir? He has excellent lines and I would like to buy him."

Elliot, taken by surprise at this remark, came forward. He wanted to say something, but didn't know what. Paolo spoke first.

"I'm sorry, but none are for sale at this time. I intend to use that one as a sire, and later on, I will sell the offspring to the soldiers."

Elliot was relieved by this remark.

"That's a shame," the officer said. "I really admire that magnificent creature. So, thank you, sir and we'll be on our way."

Paolo waved as the troopers turned and departed.

Elliot then saw Maria, who had been watching from the house. He smiled at her but she turned away.

Elliot entered the stable and placed some additional hay in Toter's stall. He petted her as she snorted.

He heard a giggle, seemingly coming from the loft. Then, gently, some hay fell about him. Curious, he went to the ladder and started up only to be confronted by Rafer. He stopped on a rung.

"Rafe, what are you doing up there?"

"I'm up here with Juanita," Rafe replied.

"Oh," Elliot said and slowly descending, chuckled to himself.

Maria walked in as Elliot turned.

"Elliot," she said, surprised. "I didn't know you were in here. I was going for a ride."

"It's kind of late to be going for a ride, ain't it?" He glanced upward, hoping Rafer and his girlfriend would not expose their presence.

Maria went to the stall where her pony was quartered.

"Can I help?" Elliot said.

"Yes, you can saddle him for me."

As he worked to cinch up the animal, he tried to think of something to say. Finishing, he handed her the reins.

"Elliot," she said softly, "I have acted like a child and ..."

"Well, I ain't been grown up about my actions, either," he interrupted.

"It's just," she continued, "I have never been close to any man, saving myself for the man I intend to marry. But, you men have the advantage. You can do anything you like — can have many women. It does not seem fair. Can you understand?"

He nodded.

"I suppose that men must do what is a natural thing while I, I must stay at home and wait." She hesitated as he moved toward her. She held her hand to his chest, stopping him.

"No, not right now," she said, and throwing the reins over her pony's mane, started to mount. "Help me up, Elliot."

He watched as she rode off.

Rafer started down the ladder and confronted him. Juanita followed, her dark tresses tangled with straw. She departed quickly after straightening her dress.

Rafer patted him on the back. "Well, it's like I said, partner, she's coming around."

"You think so? I don't know."

"Hell, you must be blind or something. I know what I'm talking about. Trust me."

"Yeah, maybe, but that ain't the end of it. There's her father to consider. If he doesn't accept me, she won't go against her father's wishes. Of this I'm sure."

"Yep, that's right. Well, let's just wait and see."

'I hope you sneaking around with that Juanita don't get you in no trouble," Elliot said, smiling at him.

"Naw," Rafer replied. "I guess I'm probably going to marry her. She's crazy about me and a bitch in bed. She's never said anything about my limp. She just enjoys being with me."

"I'm real pleased to hear that, Rafe. You deserve a good woman. Well, let's get back to work. It'll be dark soon."

That evening after supper, Billy, Rafer, and Elliot sat in front of the bunkhouse smoking and talking. Chavez was walking around, checking on the horses, and they waved to him when he passed. Then Rafer asked, "You still thinking about going to California, Billy?"

"I guess so. I like it here, but there ain't no future staying. Now, take Elliot here, he's probably gonna marry into the family and his worries is over. Me, I'm gonna mosey on come spring and see what's over them mountains there." He leaned back in his chair.

"You might find you a good woman in California," Elliot said, "and maybe settle down."

"Maybe, but I ain't in no hurry," Billy exclaimed as Rafer laughed.

When, at last, Elliot felt that his eyelids were shutting by themselves, he got up to go to bed. Billy and Rafer followed him in.

Something woke Elliot up. He had heard a noise, but thought perhaps he was dreaming. About to close his eyes again, he heard a snort. Just one of the horses, he mused, but yet he decided to investigate. Slipping on his pants, he walked out. It was a cold but clear night as he breathed in the crisp air. He stretched as he walked toward the corral. Leaning on the fence, he saw the black stallion at the other side. As he reached in his pocket to roll a cigarette, the stallion spooked. Elliot stopped and strained his eyes to see into the darkness. A figure moved beyond the far fence rail. Elliot ducked down, wondering who could be lurking in the shadows. He had not brought his gun, and without it, he felt vulnerable. Nonetheless, he had to know who it was and what he was doing skulking about.

The figure climbed inside the corral and was moving slowly. Elliot slipped into the corral as well. The horses were uneasy, milling around. Then Elliot saw him. The intruder sported the yellow leggings of a soldier. The fool is trying to steal the black horse, Elliot surmised, as he saw the man with a rope and bridle.

Elliot rushed the man and tried to tackle him, but the thief brought up the rope and slashed him across the face with it. His face stinging, Elliot turned and attacked again. As the man raised the coiled rope a second time, Elliot swung and his fist found flesh. The intruder staggered backward.

The horses bolted, trying to flee the fighting pair.

A lantern was lit in the bunkhouse as the pair wrestled on the ground. The man, on his back, kicked Elliot in the chest, knocking the breath out of him. Then he tried to flee, but Elliot tackled him again. As the man struggled to get up, he was surrounded by ranch hands, brandishing guns.

"Hold up, soldier boy," Rafer cried, holding a lantern up to his face.

Wiping the blood from his mouth, Elliot stood up and confronted him. "Damn you all to hell."

"Well, lieutenant," Billy said, "you wanted that stallion real bad, didn't you?"

"What is going on here?" Paolo yelled as he elbowed his way through the crowd. Seeing the officer, he said, "What is the meaning of this? What are you doing here?"

"He was trying to steal the black stallion, patron," Chavez said, "and Elliot here caught him at it."

Turning to the officer, Paolo said, 'Is this true, senor?"

The lieutenant said nothing, running his sleeve across his mouth.

"Do you realize the consequences of what you have done, senor?" Paolo said angrily.

Rafer leaned over and whispered in Elliot's ear, "What's that word, conse . . ., conse . . .?"

"You know that we hang horse thieves around here, lieutenant?" Chavez remarked.

"No, Chavez," Paolo interrupted, "we will not hang him. He will suffer enough when his superior hears of this. Let him go."

The others murmured negatively at this suggestion, but Paolo turned and started for the house.

"But, patron . . .," Chavez called.

Paolo, though, would not listen and continued.

Turning to the officer, Chavez said, "Consider yourself a lucky man, gringo. Now you will leave, but never come back. You will not be so lucky a second time."

"Move it," Billy said, kicking the man in the buttocks. The man fled into the night.

"He wanted that stallion so bad, he was willing to risk his career in the army," Rafer said.

"Yeah, and he lost both, too," Billy said. "You all right, Elliot?"

"Yeah, yeah, but the way I'm treated on this job, I ought to ask for a raise," he said, wiping the blood from his mouth. "I think I got a loose tooth."

14

Pete Bodine and his gang arrived at the two-story house outside of Deming. It was a small, rundown place, but a perfect hideout, he thought. There were no neighbors for miles in either direction.

Cotton Messner dismounted. He was an albino, big and white-haired. His pale eyes moved constantly not missing anything. He carried a large, wide-bladed machete on his left side. He led his horse to a water trough, then looked around. "Ain't much here."

"Who cares," Bob Hinkle said. "We ain't gonna be here for long anyways." Bob was short, bushy-haired and toted two pistols in his belt. He was staying ahead of wanted posters which dogged his trail.

Also dismounting was the only black man in the group. Beelow Hawkins was wiry, with a heavy dark mustache and close-cropped black hair. He was an ex-Yankee sharp shooter turned bad. Beelow had cut a murderous and thieving trail from Arkansas through Texas. He loosened the saddle belt and led his horse to the trough also.

"Clint," Pete called. "Check that pump at the trough and see if it's working. We need to get some fresh water." Clint Bodine was Pete's younger half-brother. He was short, like Pete, thin with a faint hint of chin stubble. He was cocky, ofttimes having to be put in his place by Pete.

"I ain't drinking no water, amigo," Tomas said angrily. "I want tequila." Tomas Melendez was a short, dirty Mexican with a huge mustache. His skin was dark and his eyebrows were so bushy, it hid his brown eyes. He wore a large sombrero with bandolier's draped across both shoulders.

"You will swill whiskey when we get this grime off of ourselves," Pete said, squinting and looking at everyone. "You stink. We all stink and I want all of you to bathe, you hear? You, Beelow, see that the horses is grained and Clint, you start cleaning up this place. It's filthy. Find a broom, anything. You, Bob, give him a hand. We may be here for a while, but when we get the word, I want us to be ready to move."

His men mumbled as they moved about to accomplish their chores.

"I didn't hire out to be no maid," Bob said.

"You had better shut up," Clint remarked, "and do as you're told. Pete ain't one to take no backtalk from nobody. Now, let's do it."

"Cotton," Pete said, "when you get done, stack some of that firewood inside. It's going to get cold." Pete noticed that there was ample provisions in the house.

The overland stagecoach pulled up at the station in Las Cruces. When the passengers disembarked, an immaculately dressed Mexican gentleman emerged. His appearance drew stares from the local populace as he extracted a handkerchief and brushed the dust from his clothes. Although thin, he stood straight and had delicate features. His ebony hair was trimmed close and slicked down.

Deputy Trent, sitting in a rocking chair on the sidewalk rose and greeted him.

"Excuse me, sir, are you looking for anyone in particular?" Trent inquired.

"Yes, the Lazy P ranchero. Is it close by?" the man replied, looking Trent up and down.

"Yessir," Trent said, pointing, "it's over in that direction. You want to go there?"

"Si, senor. Is there someone that I can hire to take me there?" He looked around with a frown on his face.

"Sure, now you just wait right here and I'll get you a rig and a driver."

"Please, I will be in that establishment there," the man said, pointing at Mason's Bar. "It has been a long trip and I'm thirsty."

The tired Mexican walked stiffly to the bar and ordered a glass of wine. As he placed the glass to his lips, he hesitated, as the aroma of it was offensive to his nose. He set the glass down firmly as a woman approached him.

"That's a mighty pretty outfit you got on, mister," she remarked.

"Why, thank you, senora."

"You just get here, on the stage, I mean?"

"Yes, senora. I have traveled a long way from Mexico City, I am here to see Senor Emilio Paolo. Do you know him?" he said, sipping the wine slowly.

"Everybody round these parts knows Mister Paolo. What's your name anyway? Mine's Jenny."

"Senora, my name is Miguel Aragon. Would it offend you if I offer to buy you a drink?" he said.

"Not at all, Mister Aragon," the woman remarked and gestured to the bartender, who responded with a bottle of whiskey and a glass. She poured a short glass full. Miguel thought it was a very strong drink for a lady.

"Do you know Mister Paolo well?" she asked.

"Frankly, no. I'm afraid I have not seen him for years, but I'm to marry his daughter, Maria."

"Oh yes, Maria. She's a pretty one all right." She turned and called over her shoulder, "Sonny, this gentleman is on his way to the Lazy P. Seems he's to marry Paolo's daughter."

Sonny, who was playing solitaire at one of the table, merely looked their way and nodded.

"You might have some competition, senor?" she said.

"I do not understand your meaning, senora?"

"Well, it ain't none of my business, but there's an hombre out at Paolo's ranch that's kind of sweet on her, seems like," Jenny whispered.

"But, that is impossible. She is betrothed to me. Our families have long ago made arrangements for this to come about. Surely, you must be mistaken."

"I could be, mind you, but I doubt it."

Deputy Trent came in and found Miguel. "Got you a buckboard, mister. You ready to go?"

Miguel tossed some coins on the counter, bowed to Jenny, and left. She followed him to the door, smiling.

"What's going on, anyway?" Sonny asked, playing a black three on a red deuce.

"Nothing, honey," she remarked, turning. "Nothing at all."

Paolo walked from the house to the corral, where Elliot and Billy were sitting on the rails.

"Amigos," Paolo hailed the two. "You still admire the horses, yes?"

Jumping down, they both said 'yes' in unison.

"Elliot here can't keep his eyes off that black stallion, senor," Billy said. "He is a beaut all right."

"Yes, he is," Paolo said. "Elliot, will you walk with me a moment? Billy, will you excuse us?"

Billy nodded and climbed back on the rail.

As they walked, Elliot noticed that Paolo had a slight limp. "What's wrong, sir?" he asked.

"Oh, it's nothing really. When the cold weather comes, my leg bothers me. Years ago, I was gored by a bull and the hurt comes back every winter. Elliot, you must know that I admire you as much as anyone. I cannot question your work and devotion, but you must understand my position regarding my only child."

"Yessir."

"And to show you of my appreciation, I will make you a present of the black stallion there, but only if you allow him to remain as a sire to the mares," Paolo concluded.

Elliot felt that this was a trade-off, a compromise of sorts — Maria for a horse. He was insulted by this remark, but remained calm.

"Senor, I appreciate your feelings, but I cannot accept the stallion. I am obligated to stay at one of the line cabins this winter, but come Spring, I will move on."

Maria then appeared before them as they rounded a corner. "Oh, father, there you are. Consuelo wanted to know what you desired for dinner this evening. Hello, Elliot."

He nodded and removed his hat.

"You may inform Consuelo that whatever she prepares will be to my liking, child."

She glanced at Elliot and was turning to leave.

"Patron?" a voice called. Paolo spun around to answer the vaquero.

"Yes, Jose, what is it?"

"Someone comes to the house," Jose said, breathlessly. "He looks like a Spanish gentleman."

Paolo started for the house flanked by Maria.

"Who can that be?" Maria asked.

Paolo stopped and strained to look, then he looked at her. "It appears to be the young Aragon, Miguel."

"That is Miguel?" she said, squinting her eyes to look at the man she was suppose to marry.

Miguel stepped gingerly down from the buckboard and dusted himself off. He looked around for someone to greet him.

"Maria," Paolo said, "please go elsewhere. I must talk to him in private."

"Father, why is he here and at this time?"

He did not answer and continued towards the visitor.

Maria watched as her father shook the man's hand and together entered the house. She turned to look at Elliot, who, in turn, turned his back on her and slowly walked away.

"Senor, I received your message and came as soon as I could. This is a dreadful country and I am very tired," Miguel remarked, wiping his nose with a laced kerchief.

"Please be seated, my boy," Paolo said, reaching for his wine decanter to pour drinks.

"Senor, is the reason I am here because someone else seeks Maria's hand in marriage?"

"That is correct, my boy, but, also I have not seen you nor your parents in many years and felt the meeting would benefit us both. And how are your parents?"

"They are well but deeply concerned about this matter."

"As I am. Please, some more wine, perhaps."

'This wine, sir, as among other things in this god-forsaken country, is not to my liking. I am anxious to resolve this problem and return to Mexico as soon as possible."

"But, my boy, should you marry my daughter, all that I have here will be yours. I want my grandchildren to live and prosper here. You must understand that this is my life and legacy."

"Senor, all that I have is in Mexico City. My father has property and concerns in a valued banking concern there and someday it will be mine."

He is a fop thought Paolo. He is not a man but a perfumed laced fop. He sat down and placed his hand on his brow.

"Perhaps, senor, after we are married, it would be better to sell this land. Maria will most certainly have more in Mexico City and will meet the most respectable gentry, which will be most suitable for all concerned. Should you like, you could certainly stay with us."

Paolo stood up, walked to his desk, retrieved a cheroot and lit it with a shaking hand. Anger was building up within him. Fleetingly, he thought of his departed wife and the promise that was made years ago regarding Maria. He had been a fool. He had insulted not only Elliot, but his daughter as well.

"May I meet Maria now, senor? I have not laid eyes on her since we were children. I would like to see the person I am to marry."

Paolo turned with smoldering eyes.

"No, young man. You may not see Maria; nor will you talk to her. You will leave my home immediately and never return. Please convey my apologies to your parents, but I cannot bless a marriage that sickens even me."

"But, senor, if I leave without Maria, how can I face my parents, my friends?"

"That, sir, is your problem. Now, leave my house and my land."

Maria was still standing outside when she saw Miguel rush out, leap into the buckboard and motion the driver to proceed. As the rig sped away, she saw her father come out, take a long puff and throw the cigar on the ground. He saw Maria and beckoned for her.

As she entered his study, he told her to sit down.

"Maria, I have been an old fool. For many years, I had dreamed of you marrying young Miguel and living here to bear my grandchildren and to continue this ranch. But, it was not meant to be. That arrogant Aragon insulted my wine, my property and my good nature. He could never be forgiven for any one of these. I should have respected your choice. Elliot is a man, a real man and a good man. I was blind, but now I see."

She ran up to him and hugged him.

"Now", he said, pulling her away. "How can I undo my insult to young Stewart?"

"I will take care of that, father," she said, smiling.

Miguel Aragon stormed into the stage depot, where he was told that the next stage south was not due for two days. Miguel paid his driver to take his belongings to the hotel. Then he returned to Mason's Bar, ordered a bottle of tequila and a glass, and found an empty table.

Jenny immediately walked over.

"Did you have some trouble at the Lazy P, Mister Aragon?" she inquired.

"Senora, please, it is of no concern to you," he said, pouring a tall drink.

Jenny moved away, but before too long, she approached him again. Miguel was now feeling quite drunk, and she began questioning him anew.

He told her that he had been insulted and readily dismissed by Paolo. Maria was not to be his wife.

"I told you, didn't I?" Jenny said.

Sonny walked over thinking that Jenny was spending too much time with this Mexican dandy.

"Sonny, this lad's been hurt. Seems Paolo run him off his place," Jenny remarked sympathetically.

"Maybe, senor," Sonny said, "I can help you."

Miguel, puzzled, replied. "And how can you help me, senor?"

"Well, if you are a mind to and got the right money, I could get Maria Paolo for you."

"What are you talking about, Sonny?" Jenny asked.

"Shush, girl, and go talk to the customers," Sonny said, looking hard at her. "I want to talk to this fine gentleman."

Later that evening, while preparing for bed, Jenny cornered Sonny, asking him what had happened between he and the Mexican.

"Miguel wants someone to kidnap Maria Paolo so he can take her back to Mexico City. Once she is in Mexico, custom would prevent him for being at fault and she'll have to marry him."

"You put him up to this, didn't you?"

"Well, I could sure use five thousand dollars right now," he said, smiling broadly.

"Five thou ..." She gasped, then summoned a wry smile.

"Plus the fact, honey," he continued, "it gets her out of the way."

"You're a devil, you are," she said.

15

Maria asked Juanita to summon Chavez to her in the dining room. A few moments later, Chavez, hat in hand, walked in.

"You wanted me, senorita?"

"Yes, Chavez, old friend, I want you to do me a favor," she said grinning. "This afternoon, I intend to go riding by myself."

"I'll have a vaquero saddle your horse, Chiquita," he interrupted.

"Let me finish, please. I will be riding to the east range. You know where the line cabin is near the big pine tree?"

"Si, senorita."

"I want you to send Elliot to that place on some pretense of work - comprende?"

"I understand perfectly, senorita, but what about Consuelo?"

"Forget Consuelo," she said, "she has enough to do. At last my father has seen the true Miguel Aragon and he has concluded that Elliot is the right one."

"I agree, senorita. Senor Stewart is a strong vaquero and I, for one, trust him." "Yes, I do, too, so long as he does not wander to Las Cruces for awhile."

Elliot could not understand why Chavez wanted him to look for strays on the east range. After all, as far as he knew, all of the cattle

149

had been accounted for, yet orders were orders. It was cold as he rode Toter slowly eastward.

After several miles, he came to one of the line shacks. A wisp of smoke arose from the chimney. Now, who could that be, he thought. All of the wranglers were at the ranch. Perhaps a passerby decided to get out of the cold. Anyway, he had to investigate. At the entrance, he dismounted, drew his pistol and slowly unlatched the door. Stepping in he saw Maria facing the stove. Then she turned and smiled.

"Maria, what are you doing way out here by yourself?" he asked, surprised.

"Waiting for you," she demurred.

"Hmm, did you and Chavez cook this up? Sending me way out to nowhere for no good reason?"

"It was for a good reason, Elliot." She slowly walked up to him, cupped his face in her hands and softly kissed him.

She explained her father's actions regarding the meeting with young Aragon, his regrets and his esteem for Elliot.

"Oh, and father still wants you to have the black stallion, my sweet," she said.

They kissed and then sat by the fire for a little while.

Near dark, he doused the fire and accompanied her back to the ranch.

Consuelo was relieved when she returned.

After breakfast, the cowhands gathered outside amid falling snow-flakes. They huddled close pulling their fur-lined collars up around their napes.

Chavez paired up the cowhands who were to inhabit the line cab-ins. Rafer and Elliot were to man the northern cabin on the boundary with the Simpson spread. They would watch the cattle belonging to the remaining Simpson girl as well as Paolo's animals, so their range was now greater than the other cowhands.

After receiving their assignment, they packed their belongings and went to the stable to saddle their horses. A few moments elapsed when Elliot looked up and saw Maria standing in the doorway. Rafe, following his gaze, also saw her. He hurriedly cinched up his pony and said that he would wait for Elliot outside. Passing Maria, he doffed his hat.

Maria ran to Elliot and kissed him.

"My father said that come spring and upon your return, we can be married," she said, kissing him again.

"I don't know how a man can be so lucky," he said, looking down at her. "A few months ago, I was a down-and-out drifter, no job, no nothing. Now, I finally got you. I can't ask for anymore, Maria."

"But, in your absence, my sweet," she demurred, "you may change your mind about marrying me."

"Do you think I'm crazy? Hell, girl, there ain't a man within a thousand miles that wouldn't give his right arm for you."

"Am I so beautiful?" she said, teasing him.

"Listen, Maria, if another man so much as makes a move on you, I ..."

She put her fingers to his lips to quiet him. Then she kissed him again.

"Come on, Elliot!" Rafer yelled from the barn door.

Outside, Elliot slowly mounted his horse, "You take care of my new black horse, you hear?"

Billy, who was to remain at the ranch house, waved as Elliot and Rafer headed north.

"Well," Rafer exclaimed, 'looks like you and the senorita are gonna get hitched after all. Didn't I tell you? I know women."

"You sure do, partner," Elliot replied, smiling.

"Seems to me if you was so tight with her now, you could've asked them to let us stay at the main house and let some other cowpokes stay at the line cabin and freeze to death."

"Listen, Rafe. I'm not about to mess things up right now. I don't have a problem being at the line cabin. At least I can't be accused of being with a woman up there," Elliot said laughing.

"Well, if you're gonna marry the senorita, then I ain't gonna be left alone. I think I'll just marry my little Mexican filly."

"Hey, Rafe, that's great news. I'm happy for you."

"Might's well," Rafe continued. "I think she's carrying my child anyway."

"Why, you old son-of-a-gun, you," Elliot said. "Ain't that something."

They both rode along laughing and punching one another playfully.

16

Miguel Aragon made straight for the telegraph office and sent a message to the Nationale Bank of Mexico. It was a request for funds to be transferred to the local bank in Las Cruces. Then he went to Mason's Bar, to find Sonny.

"Senor Mason," Miguel said, "how do you intend to do this thing?"

'There's no need for you to stick around, Miguel," Sonny said. "If we grab Miss Paolo, the sheriff will get suspicious with you hanging around. If you don't mind, I'm going to direct you to a hideout I've got, and when it's done, give you an escort to Mexico City. Is that all right?"

"Si, Senor Mason. I do not like to do this thing, but I cannot allow my betrothed to marry another. I and my family would be insulted, you understand," Miguel said.

Sonny looked around the bar and smiled as he saw Devon sitting in the corner.

"Devon," he called, "come here a minute, will you?"

Devon, holding his drink, walked over and sat down.

"Devon, you want another job?" he asked.

Devon nodded, checking Aragon out. "Okay, go find Rusty Murtaugh for me and come back." Devon gulped down his drink and left.

"Miguel, why don't you go to the hotel and stay there until we are ready. Here, take this bottle of tequila with you," Sonny said, shoving a bottle toward him. Miguel carefully took the bottle and departed.

Sonny glanced around when the door banged shut. Devon was following Rusty Murtaugh into the saloon. He directed them to come into his office and closed the door when they entered.

"Rusty, you want to get even with that Elliot fella, don't you? Well, you can do it and get paid for it at the same time. What do you say?" Sonny said.

"What do I have to do?" Murtaugh replied.

"I've got Pete Bodine and his gang holed up, and they're gonna help me take over the Lazy P. You can join them and get your revenge at the same time," Sonny said.

"What about me, Mr. Mason?" Devon asked.

"Oh yeah, Devon, you're hired, too. We got enough guns behind us to really get the job done right. Now, you two have a drink and I'll be right back."

Sonny returned in a few moments, holding some papers.

"Now, Rusty, go over to the hotel and tell that Mexican, Aragon, to go with you and Devon. Here is a map on how to get to the hideout. You give this note to Bodine. I'd better get you a case of whiskey to take with you. Those boys will get mighty nervous to have something to do quickly, and I'm not quite ready. You understand now?"

Rusty nodded, took the papers, and the two departed.

"Someone comes," Tomas called to the others, while gazing out the window. The other occupants joined him.

"There's only three of them," Pete said. "You stay inside, I'll talk to them."

He put on his gun belt, and checking the chamber, slowly walked out.

The three riders reined up.

"You Pete Bodine?" the biggest of the men called out.

"Do I know you?" Pete said, his hand near his pistol.

"I'm Rusty Murtaugh, and I got a note for you from Sonny Mason."

Pete eyed each man then said, "Step down and come on in."

One of the men carried in a case of whiskey, which the others quickly opened it up, while Rusty gave Bodine the note. After reading it, he told everyone to settle down as he needed to go to Las Cruces alone.

Elliot and Rafer quickly settled into their temporary home. They took their time dusting and cleaning the premises while also checking the cattle daily. A lean-to on the east side of the cabin was used to quarter their animals against the bitter cold that soon would descend upon them.

Elliot chopped the firewood and stacked it in the cabin. He thought that it would be a long spell before he could savor the sweet jasmine perfume that surrounded Maria, and he suddenly realized that he was now glad that he had not married Mary Louise.

Rafer did most of the cooking. He did not like the cold, which bothered his leg, so he chose to remain as close to the cookstove as he could. He would alternate preparing beans, bacon, beef, and boiled corn. Once in awhile, when available, they would dine on roasted rabbit or peccary.

In the evenings, they would only light one lantern to conserve kerosene and sit around talking while smoking roll-your-owns. In order to stay warm, they would go to bed early, placing several blankets over themselves.

By mid-December, the weather had turned bitterly cold. Elliot noticed snow on top of the Sacramento Mountains, far to the north. Every other day he would mount Toter and range far, trying to keep tabs on the cattle, which often strayed into the brush to take cover from the extreme cold. One night it snowed so hard he could not find his way back to the cabin and sought shelter in a pine grove. Ripping boughs off the trees, he buried himself in them but suffered miserably even with a fire burning.

The next morning, he resumed his trek back to the cabin. Snow swirled endlessly when he suddenly came upon a figure kneeling in the snow. The man, startled by his appearance, leaped up with a bloody knife in his hand. It was an Indian and he was butchering a steer.

The two stared at one another.

Elliot knew that the Indian, afoot, could not move towards him fast enough before he could draw his pistol so he held up his hand in a peace sign.

155

"You speak American?" he asked.

"Yes," the Indian replied.

"I don't mean you any harm so lower your knife," he called out. As the Indian dropped his hand, Elliot dismounted and walked towards him.

"That's a whole lot of meat you got there. Is it for your family?" he inquired, pointing at the carcass.

"It is for my tribe, white man. My people are hungry and the buffalo are no longer here," the Indian replied, shifting nervously.

"I understand. Tell you what? You cut me a piece of that hindquarter there so's I can have some beef, and you can go on your way. Is that fair enough?"

The Indian smiled, turned and deftly separated some of the steer's leg and held it up for him. Elliot took the leg and tied it to his saddle. Reaching in his saddle bag, he took out a pouch of tobacco and began rolling a cigarette. Wetting the paper and finishing, he handed it to the Indian and began making another. They talked while smoking.

The Indian informed him that his tribe was located a half-day's ride and numbered some twenty souls. He was a proud mescalero and did not like to steal but had no choice. His people were starving and as an elder he was duty bound to find sufficient food.

"You ride for senor Paolo?" the Indian asked.

Elliot nodded.

"Then you know Two-Horse."

"Harry? Sure, I know him," Elliot said.

'Two-Horse and me blood kin."

"Well, how about that? Yep, Harry is a good friend," Elliot said. "Listen, I'll tell him next time I see him that I ran into you. What's your name anyway?"

"I am called Untula."

"I'm glad to know you, Untula. I'd best be on my way before I freeze to death," Elliot said, mounting. "Make sure you don't damage my fence when you leave."

The Indian nodded and watched as Elliot waved and rode away.

It was night as Pete Bodine snuck into town and knocked on the backdoor of Mason's Bar. Once inside, he demanded an explanation from Sonny about the extra people he had to put up with, plus the change of plans. Sonny, calming him, explained that with more gunmen, it might go easier.

"Tell me why we need to kidnap the Paolo girl?" Pete inquired. "I'm just not into that sort of thing."

"Listen, there's an extra thousand in it for you if you get the girl and take her and Aragon to Mexico," Sonny mentioned.

"Well, I could use the extra money. Okay, it's a deal. Now, is this Devon Mitchell any good with a gun?"

"I don't know, but he knows the Lazy P ranch house and he could use a job. Now, Rusty's got a beef with one of the ranch hands whose name is Elliot Stewart. He'll fit in with your bunch because he aches to kill Stewart."

"So, when do I start?" Pete said. "My boys are anxious to make some money."

"I heard that the Lazy P hands are already split up, so you can start anytime, but keep me informed."

"Oh, about the sheriff," Pete continued, "I don't want to be doing my job and have him breathing down my neck. It would be better if we got rid of him first."

Sonny rose up. "Do what you have to do. I ain't crazy about Gentry anyhow."

Opening the door, Pete melted into the night.

"Going after the Lazy P ain't going to be easy, honey," Jenny remarked, walking up.

"Maybe not, but I'm going to try," he said.

"Well, I want Bodine to make sure he gets rid of that Elliot Stewart character," she said.

"Huh? What do you know about this man Stewart?" Turning to her angrily, he stared hard. "You have a run-in with him, or did you try to bed him down? Tell me."

"No, honey, really. He just talked bad to me, that's all, honest."

"You're lying, Jenny," he said and backhanded her across the face. She staggered backwards into the wall.

Pointing a finger at her, he shouted, "One day, so help me, I'm going to catch you thumping a damned cowboy and cut your face so's nobody will look at you twice, you hear? Now, you mind the bar and keep your damn bloomers on."

She rubbed her face, hate in her eyes.

17

Tom Gentry, bundled up warmly, hesitated before leaving his office for the nightly ritual of checking doors. The night was cold, and he stopped to chat with Trent, who was stoking the pot-bellied stove, before deciding he could delay no longer.

The town was quiet enough, much to his liking. Tom was due to retire soon, having been sheriff for many years. He thought of how relaxing it would be for him not to have to shake any more doors in the dead of winter as he stopped to fire up his pipe. His face was bathed in the light as a shot rang out. Clenching his teeth tightly, the stem of his pipe broke as a slug hit him full in the chest. He grunted and crumpled to the sidewalk and lay still.

Faintly, he heard horses galloping away, but the sound was swallowed up in the night.

A moment later, Trent was at his side, rolling him over.

"Tom, are you hit bad? What happened?" he shouted, holding Tom's head up.

Tom gasped for breath. "God damn it, Trent, I been hit! Get me to the doc fast before I pass out."

Trent helped Tom to his feet as the sheriff held his chest and coughed hoarsely.

Trent rousted the doctor, who sleepily cleared his table to admit him. They both helped Tom get out of his heavy parka, then gently lowered him onto the table. The doctor quickly examined him, and finding little blood, probed further.

"Tom, you got real lucky, son," the doctor sighed. "That heavy coat saved your life. You got a broken rib and you're gonna be laid up for a few days, but you'll be all right. I'll just give you something for the pain."

Snow blanketed the ground as the cowboys tried to stay indoors at the ranch. Most of the time was spent feeding the animals and cutting up firewood.

Maria busied herself by fitting some of her clothes for young Carol. Consuelo helped by pinning dress lengths and sewing. Maria was pleased to have Carol there. They talked incessantly especially of the future,

"One day, Carol," Maria said, "you will be able to take over your father's ranch and marry a strong man who will work it right for you."

"Maybe someone like mister Stewart?" Carol remarked, giggling.

"Maybe, that is, if you're lucky."

"He's a nice man, isn't he?"

"Yes."

"Tell me about Billy? What's he like?" Carol inquired.

"Billy? Oh, he's all right I suppose," Maria exclaimed, "but, I'm afraid he has the wandering fever. He probably won't stay here after winter."

Consuelo, sewing a dress looked up. "Senorita, I am running out of thread and ribbon. I cannot finish."

"Well," Maria said, staring at Carol. "We'll just have to get some more. I know it's cold but would you like to go to Las Cruces and shop?"

"Could we? I would love to get out for awhile and," she said, "could we go by our place and visit my father's grave?"

"Yes. I will speak to my father."

"Okay, fellas, we'd best get moving," Pete said, "so, let's pack up. Senor Aragon, you will stay here. We should be back in three or four days and we'll have your girl friend with us."

The group began saddling their horses.

"Rusty?" Pete said, "you and Beelow scout the Paolo ranch. If you have a chance, get the girl. If not, we'll see you near the north end after we take care of the hands at the line shacks. There won't be many that could stop us and we'll rush the place. Let's go."

The group split up and departed.

"Chavez," Maria remarked, "my father said that Carol and myself could go to Las Cruces. Would you see to a buckboard for us?"

"Si, senorita, but it's cold and you must dress warmly." Chavez turned and went to the bunkhouse. Entering, he commanded two of his Mexican cowhands to get a buckboard ready — one will drive and the other will follow.

Within minutes, they were at the ranch entrance. Maria and Carol emerged and were helped into the rig. Paolo waved to them as they left.

Maria pulled a blanket over their legs as they talked and laughed. It had been a long time since they had been away from the confines of the house and they enjoyed the outing.

The following vaquero constantly swept the horizon with his eyes.

"When we return," Maria said, "we will go by your ranch and then stop long enough for me to see Elliot. Do you mind?"

"No, I don't mind, Maria," Carol replied.

"Anyway, if it's dark, we'll just stay at their cabin for the night."

They had been riding for awhile when they saw two riders approaching. Maria tried to recognize the riders and finally recognized one of them. He had spoken to her in Las Cruces. She became uncomfortable as the rider's neared.

The driver brought up a rifle as he turned to check his rearguard compatriot.

The men drew up in front of the carriage preventing the driver from continuing.

"Good afternoon, ladies," Murtaugh said, removing his hat and smiling. "It's a cold day for a ride, ain't it?"

His companion, Beelow, did not utter a word but closely watched the driver and the outrider.

"Amigo, I remember you," Maria said. "You spoke to me in Las Cruces, didn't you?"

"I did for a fact, m'am," Rusty said. "I'm flattered you remembered." He looked beyond the buckboard. "Who is that following you people?"

The driver turned around to look and Maria was stunned as the black man drew his pistol and shot him. The blast was deafening. Carol screamed as the wounded driver pitched forward out of the buckboard. The vaquero in the rear brought his gun up but Rusty shot him in the shoulder. The vaquero dropped his pistol and turning his pony, galloped off.

"Go get him, Beelow," Rusty shouted as he grabbed the reins of the team.

Beelow kicked his horse's flanks and sped away. Shortly, he returned saying he was unable to catch the fleeing Mexican.

"It don't matter," Rusty said. "We got what we came for. Here, you drive the buckboard and let's get out of here."

"What about the young'un? We gonna take her, too?" Beelow asked, tying his mount on the rear of the rig and climbing aboard.

"Hell no. She can get down and walk for all I care. That one there is the one we want," Rusty said, pointing at Maria.

Carol stood alone, sobbing as the others rode off. Maria, beside Beelow, looked back at her, but said nothing. She was powerless to do anything.

"Did you hear that?" Rafer said, looking south.

"Yeah," Elliot said, "it was a gunshot, and not too far away either. You get some more firewood in the cabin, Rafe, and I'll mosey on over in that direction and have a looksee. We ain't supposed to have any people over there. Could be an Indian shooting another steer."

After about a mile of riding and turning his head often, Elliot could not see a thing. He thought that perhaps the gunshot was further east; and as he was about to change directions, he spotted a wisp of smoke in the distance. Hitting his horse's flanks hard, he felt the cool wind biting his face as he sped toward the scene.

As he came closer, he saw a girl standing next to a mesquite bush that was on fire. He realized that it was Carol, and then saw a Mexican lying on the ground beside her. He seemed dead. Elliot quickly dismounted and ran to Carol.

"Miss Simpson, what happened?"

Between sobs, she related the events to him. As he took in the words, his mind tried to figure out why the gunmen would only take Maria and not young Carol. Could they want her as a hostage? Paolo was well known in these parts and loved his daughter dearly. That must be it, he thought. They might trade her for money.

He removed the dead man's jacket and bundled Carol up with it to ward off the chill. Then he put her up on his horse, and mounting himself, rode toward the Lazy P. On the way, he asked Carol to describe the abductors. When she mentioned the black man, he felt that he wouldn't be hard to locate. There weren't many black people in this country. But at her description of the white man, his breath seemed sucked away. It fit Murtaugh to a tee. If they so much as touched Maria, he would go crazy. Thinking the worst, he raked his mare's flank vigorously. He did not have the time to get word back to Rafer, but decided he could handle things until he got back.

As they arrived back at the ranch, Paolo ran out, excited as he saw Carol with him but not Maria.

"What is wrong, Elliot?" Paolo cried. "Where is Maria?"

Handing Carol into Billy's waiting arms, he said, "Some hombres took her, senor, and they rode west. They killed the driver, but I know who they are. I'll get her back."

"Why do they do this thing?" Paolo lamented, teary-eyed.

"Probably hold her for ransom. Billy, where's Harry?"

"He and Chavez are at the eastern line shack. They won't be back for at least three hours," Billy said. "Hell, I'll go with you."

"No, you stay here because I need to get word to Rafe anyway. When Harry gets back, send him north and he can pick up the buckboard trail. I'll try to be in front of him and he can join me. You got that?" Elliot shouted. "Jose, cut me out a fresh horse. My mare's beat."

"Si, Senor Elliot," Jose said, turning toward the corral.

Dismounting, Elliot loosened the saddle and pulled it off his trusted mare. Even with the cold, she was lathered and needed a rubdown, food, and warmth.

"You say you know who these men are?" Paolo inquired.

"Yessir, the big one's named Rusty Murtaugh. His brother was killed and I know he blames me for it."

Paolo placed his hands on Elliot's shoulders.

"Elliot, I'm counting on you. Do not let these gringos harm my daughter, but should they want money ..."

"They ain't gonna get no money, senor, because they ain't gonna be able to spend it," Elliot said, his eyes on fire.

Jose brought another horse and Elliot hastily placed his saddle on it's back, mounted, and sped away.

"Vaya con Dios, my son," Paolo shouted.

"Well, old girl," Rafer said, leaning over the bloated cow, "let's see about your young'un."

Carefully he ran his hand up into the cow's uterus and felt around. Pulling his arm out, he patted the pained animal.

"Everything's gonna be all right, but I'll stay here with you until he decides to want to come out. But he better hurry up, it's gonna get cold by nightfall."

He heard riders approaching. Standing up he thought it might be Elliot and somebody else. As the riders drew nearer, he counted four and recognized one of them.

"Hey, Devon," he called, "what're you doing way out here?" But before he received an answer, a volley of gunshots tore into him. A puzzled look swept over his face as he looked down at the blood on this chest. Then he looked up at Devon, who had not drawn his gun. Slowly, his eyes rolled back and he pitched forward.

"Where's his partner anyway?" Clint asked.

"Maybe he's back at the cabin now. Anyway you'd better find him before he finds out about Rafer here," Devon said, looking down at the still form of Rafer. He felt sick.

The group turned and left the scene.

When Elliot reached the cabin, he noticed that Rafer's horse was gone. Figuring that Rafer was out checking the cattle and that he needed to go after Maria, he went inside to leave a note. As he walked out the door to mount his horse, a shot rang out and he tumbled to the ground.

18

It seemed like hours had passed when Elliot awoke. Reaching up, he felt blood on his temple. Finally, he was able to roll over and sit up, his head throbbing. He tried to figure out what had happened He had not seen nor heard anyone, and Rafer — where was Rafer? As he regained his senses, he became more concerned about his absent partner. His horse was standing nearby, pawing the ground. Slowly, Elliot stood up, but then fell backward. He tried again and managed to shake the fog from his brain enough to stand.

Reaching for his horse's reins, he slowly pulled himself up and settled in the saddle. Turning the horse, he moved slowly away. It was not long when he found Rafer's horse tied to a small bush. Looking around, he saw his partner, blood surrounding him. Dismounting, he stumbled toward Rafer and knelt beside him. Turning Rafer over, tears welled in his eyes.

The bitter wind chilled him as he sadly buried his partner. Then, lifting his head toward heaven, he asked the almighty to receive Rafer graciously.

Although his senses were numb, he vowed that he would avenge Rafer's senseless killing.

Going back to the cabin, he stumbled in, tired and hurt. He sat down for a moment, thinking of Rafer and Maria. She was now his prime concern but first, he had to gain some of his strength back. Time was precious and he dared not sleep but he laid his head down on the table. His mind drifted, half in sleep until he jerked up upon hearing the door latch. He fumbled for his gun only to see Harry Two-Horse enter, also with gun drawn.

"Harry, thank God you're here," Elliot said, clumsily standing.

"Elliot, I told you a long time ago it was coming, didn't I? Well, it's here," Harry said.

"Maria's been kidnapped and Rafe's dead. I don't know what's going on, Harry. Nobody had call to kill Rafer. He never hurt nobody."

Harry didn't reply as he wrapped a bandage around Elliot's head wound. Elliot was so angry he was shaking.

"I'm sorry about Rafer, Elliot. There is little justice west of the Pecos," Harry said, 'Very little. Can you ride?"

"Hell yes, I can ride." He walked forward unsteadily.

"Then let's move."

Beelow, driving the buckboard with Maria seated beside him, pulled up in front of the hideout. He escorted Maria into the house and she was surprised at what greeted her.

"Miguel, is that you?" she said. "What do these gringos want with us?"

"Senorita Maria," Miguel confessed, "they brought you here at my request. Had you forgotten that we were to be married? You and your father shamed my family's name and I could not allow that."

"You mean that these murderers are working for you?" Maria said, unbelievingly.

"Yes, and I paid them very well," Miguel said.

She walked over to him and viciously slapped him across his face. "You fool, do you know what you have done? These men have killed our people."

Cotton, witnessing this tirade, laughed. "She's a real spitfire, ain't she?"

More horses rode up as Rusty looked out the window.

Pete came in, followed by the others. He poured himself a drink.

"You, I know you," Maria said, upon seeing Devon Mitchell.

Devon cast his eyes downward, as if ashamed.

"You ate in my home. You were paid good money and you were asked to remain with us, and this is how you repay our kindness. What kind of man are you?" Maria said, standing arrogantly in front of him. "When Elliot finds out. .."

Devon looked up, straight into her face. "Elliot's dead, and so's his partner, Rafer."

"What?" Maria exclaimed. "You're lying."

"No, he ain't lying, miss," Pete interjected. "Now, get over there, sit down, and be quiet."

"You tell her," Clint said, grinning.

"Senor Bodine," Miguel said, "now that I have Maria, I would like an escort to Mexico as soon as possible."

"Okay, but I can only spare one person. We still got a lot of work to do, and I'm gonna need all my men." He looked around. "Tomas, you know the country well. You take them."

"Are we going after the ranch now?" Clint said.

Turning to him, Pete was visibly angry. "Shut your damn face, Clint. You talk too much. Now let's get moving."

As they readied to depart, Pete pulled Miguel aside. 'Tell me, Mister Aragon, just how much did you pay Mason for us to get the girl?"

"Five thousand Yankee dollars."

"Why that no-good . . . okay, on your way. Tomas, take them just across the border and hightail it back as soon as you can."

Maria, with tears in her eyes, got on the buckboard, then turned back to Miguel. "When my father finds out about your betrayal, he will not rest until you have paid for it."

"He should not have betrayed me, Maria. I could not go back to Mexico City without you."

Closely following the buckboard ruts, Harry said, "Elliot, it's no problem to follow this trail, but we are going to need help. Deming is in that direction." He pointed west. "That is the way I'm heading. It's only a few miles to Las Cruces. Sidetrack there and get the sheriff and a posse. He owes us anyway. You can cross my trail and I'll be waiting for you."

"But, Maria . . ." Elliot said.

"They won't harm her, I'm sure. Just go and get some help. There's too many of them."

Elliot raked his horse's flanks and galloped away.

After what seemed like a lifetime, Elliot finally arrived in Las Cruces and headed for the sheriffs office. Bursting inside, he saw the deputy sitting behind the sheriff's desk.

"Where's the sheriff, Foster?" Elliot said breathlessly.

"Hell, Stewart, he's laid up. He was shot the other night out there on the street." Then, seeing the neckerchief wrapped around Elliot's head, he said, "What happened to you, anyway?"

"We got troubles at the Lazy P. We got three dead already and Lord knows what's happened at the other line cabins. We got to have some help, deputy, and quick."

"My Lord, you'd think the Lincoln County Wars had come here, man," Foster said, rising up.

"Deputy, I don't have time to palaver, I need a posse. Now, we got any shooters in this town?"

"Elliot, I can't gather a posse without Tom's authorization," Foster lamented.

"Dammit, Foster, then take me to the sheriff."

They both walked briskly toward the sheriff's home. They found him in bed, resting.

Elliot explained the situation to the sheriff and Tom's mind seemed to be racing.

"You know, Elliot," he said, "I have a gut feeling that Bodine's tied up in this somehow."

"Bodine, I heard that name somewhere," Elliot said, adjusting the neckerchief on his head.

"Pete Bodine is a shootist for hire. A few weeks ago, he and five others rode in, stopped at Mason's for a drink, and left, They told me they was just passing through, and I ain't seen them since. But I'll bet my last dollar that Mason's behind this whole thing. Yeah, and that's why I was shot, to get me out of the way. Makes sense now."

"Mason, you say, huh?" Elliot said. "Sheriff, give Foster the authority to round up a posse and I'll meet them in front of your office."

"Where're you going?" Tom asked.

"I need a drink," he said angrily, and stormed out.

As he entered Mason's, he paid no attention to two patrons at the bar, but made straight for the office. The bartender tried to stop him, but Elliot backhanded him full across the nose. The bartender grabbed his face and backpedaled, cursing.

The office door opened and Jenny stepped out. "What the hell is ... ?" She stopped when she saw Elliot.

"What's the matter, Jenny, you look like you've just seen a ghost?" Elliot said.

Recovering quickly, she said, "No, no, I was just wondering what happened to your head."

"Pulling off his hat, Elliot tore off the temporary bandage and tossed it on the floor.

Sonny Mason suddenly entered from the office.

"Well, if it ain't your husband," Elliot remarked with a wry grin.

"You're Stewart, ain't you?" Sonny said, standing next to Jenny.

"Yeah, I'm Stewart," he said, looking around. "Where're your friends right now?"

"What friends you talking about?" Sonny asked.

"I mean Bodine and his guns," Elliot declared.

At the mention of Bodine's name, Sonny stiffened and Elliot noticed it.

"Bodine? Bodine? Oh yeah, he was here a long time ago, but he and his friends headed north. What's he got to do with me anyway?"

"When I find out, Sonny, I'll be back. You can count on it. You see, they made some bad mistakes," Elliot remarked, leering at Sonny. "They killed my partner and took my girl."

"It's a pity they didn't kill you, too," Jenny said.

"Shut up, Jenny," Sonny shouted, then he turned back to Elliot and continued. "Look, I'm sorry about your partner, but I ain't involved in whatever it is you're talking about, cowboy,"

Elliot slowly walked behind the counter and poured himself a drink. The bartender backed away, still holding his bloody nose. Looking hard at the Masons, Elliot downed the drink and turned for the door.

Reaching the entrance, he turned and yelled. "Remember what I said." Noticing he still had the whiskey glass in his hand, he tossed it over the counter smashing into bottles.

Sonny, shoving Jenny back into his office, shouted at the bartender. "Dammit, you're bleeding all over the floor. Get a rag."

Slamming the door, he berated Jenny for her untimely and stupid outburst.

Elliot returned to the sheriff's office. There were four men standing near the desk.

"Elliot, these were all the men I could muster," Foster said, "and I'd like to go with you, but with Tom laid up. ... "

"I know," Elliot said. "Can you fellas shoot, I mean, shoot good? Because we're going up against professionals."

They all nodded.

"You paying for us to ride, mister?" one of the men said.

Elliot looked at him hard, then at Trent.

"Fine bunch of upstanding citizens you got here, deputy," he said.

Foster shrugged his shoulders.

"My friend," Elliot explained, "I ain't got no money, but I'll see that each of you will get paid for your troubles. Now, let's mount up."

The others walked out in front of Elliot.

"Elliot, can I see you a minute before you go?" Foster remarked.

"What is it?" Elliot asked, shutting the door. "I'm in a damned hurry."

"I know he wasn't supposed to tell me, but the telegraph operator came in a few minutes ago. Seems that the fancy Mexican that came in a day or two ago wired Mexico City for money."

"Go on," Elliot said.

"It was five thousand dollars and he saw the Mex hand it over to Sonny Mason."

Elliot spun around. "So, they're all tied into it together, eh? Sonny, Bodine and that Aragon dandy. He don't want no ransom money because he's gonna take Maria to Mexico. Sure, it's all coming together now. Thanks, Foster, and I need another favor from you."

"What's that?"

"Keep an eye on Sonny and that no-good wife of his. I've got a score to settle with them two sidewinders."

170

"Whatever you say, Elliot."

He hurried outside and mounted. The posse members were already waiting for him to lead them out of town.

The posse picked up the trail where Elliot had split off from Harry earlier. By late that evening, they caught up with him. He was sitting under a tree, smoking a cigarette. Getting up and stretching, he said, "Is that all the posse you could get together? Where's the sheriff and the deputy?"

Elliot told him about the sheriff's plight.

"Now, what've we got here?" Elliot asked.

"They were holed up in that house over yonder," Harry said, pointing, "but they've already left. Come, I want to show you something."

He led them to the front of the house and knelt down. "Look," he declared, pointing south. "The buckboard has gone south with a riderless horse tied to the back, and these tracks, seven in all, are heading back east."

'It's just as I figured," Elliot said. "They are taking Maria to Mexico. That Aragon's probably with her."

"Yeah, and the driver, because his horse is tied on back, is coming back, too," Harry declared. "But it's the others I'm more worried about, Elliot. Why didn't they go south as well. I'm afraid they may be headed back toward the Lazy P."

"Well, I'm going after Maria," Elliot said, "and the rest of you follow the others."

"Listen, amigo," Harry said, "it is dark. They will stop for the night, too. We may as well sleep under a roof and get a couple hours of rest. We can start fresh at daylight."

Harry entered the house first, with Elliot right behind.

"Smell that, Elliot?"

"Yeah, jasmine," he replied, "and whiskey and sweat."

Elliot could not sleep as his mind was racing, worrying about Maria. He didn't think any harm would befall her, but he couldn't rest easy until she was safe with him.

They were up before dawn and quickly mounted to leave.

"I'll join you fellas as soon as I get Maria back," Elliot shouted as he headed south.

19

Bodine and his henchmen rode up, facing another line cabin. The two Mexican hands slowly walked out of the cabin and were immediately cut down by gunfire. One cowboy was still writhing on the ground as Cotton dismounted and slowly walked up to him with a drawn machete. He smiled as he brought it down. Devon, sickened by this callous display, turned his head.

"Dammit, Pete, this is going too far," he said. "I ain't got no stomach for this. I'm getting out of here."

Pete looked at him, smiling slightly. "I figured it was going to come to this, Mitchell, but I ain't got no money to pay you off, so ..."

'To hell with the money," Devon replied, looking at the others, "I'm headed north like I should've a long time ago."

"Suit yourself," Pete remarked, winking at Clint.

Devon turned his pony, but Clint, still with his gun in his hand, raised up and shot him in the back.

"Now, he don't have to worry about his stomach anymore, does he?" Clint said, holstering his gun.

"Hey Pete," Cotton said, "why are we fooling around? There can't be a half-dozen hands left at the Lazy P ranch house. Let's go there and finish the job."

"Yeah, Pete," Clint agreed, "I'm all for that. We can take them easy, get our money, and be done with it."

"Well, that ain't what we were supposed to do, but it's not a bad idea," Pete said, pondering. "Okay, we'll do it."

Elliot found the trail easy enough to follow, and he could cover more ground than the slower buckboard. He should be able to catch up to them in a couple of hours, he thought. His horse, however, soon became winded by the spurring of his determination, so, Elliot was forced to walk him for a few minutes.

Once they started into a gallop again, it wasn't long before Elliot spotted the buckboard and its occupants. The driver had set a leisurely pace at Miguel's insistence, making it easier for Elliot. He needed to get in front of them, so he made a wide sweep around them, unseen. Finally, he took a position behind some rocks and waited. When the buckboard was getting nearer, he noticed a Mexican driving, with Aragon sitting beside him. Maria was alone in the back seat.

Cocking his pistol, he stepped out.

"Pull up," he shouted.

The Mexican stood up and reached for his pistol, but Elliot's gun flashed and the slug caught him in the throat. He fell backwards into Maria's lap, and Miguel put his hands up.

"Elliot," Maria shouted, "they told me you were dead." She jumped off the rig and rushed to him.

"You, Aragon," he said, "off the wagon."

"Please, Elliot, do not shoot him," she cried.

"I ain't gonna shoot him, Maria, but he has to pay," Elliot said, watching as Aragon got down.

"He will pay, Elliot," Maria whispered. "When my father tells his family what he has done, he will be disowned and kicked out. He will have nothing."

Elliot looked at her then at Miguel.

"You're damned lucky I don't pistol whip you," Elliot said.

"Senor," Miguel pleaded, "I did not know that Senor Mason was trying to get Paolo's ranchero, but I know now."

"Hell, mister, I already knew that. He'll pay too. Now, you ain't that far from Mexico, so start walking and never show your face around here again."

"But, senor, I will freeze. Please, leave me a horse," Miguel begged.

Ignoring him, Elliot picked Maria up and placed her in the buckboard and started back north. Maria turned and looked backward sadly.

Elliot told her of Rafer's killing. She was saddened by it all.

"How many are down there?" Clint asked of Pete as they looked down on the ranch house.

"All I can see is five men," Pete said, "but let's give it another minute to make sure."

"Only five?" Rusty commented. "Hell, that ain't no problem. Let's rush them."

"Just hold on, Rusty, I'm running this show," Pete said irritably.

Paolo walked out of the house and was seen speaking to Billy.

"That must be the boss," Beelow commented. 'That's six in all."

"Okay, let's go, spread out but keep low until we can get into position, then we rush them," Pete said.

They started down the slope.

"What is that?" the ranch hand said. He stared in the distance as Billy sauntered up.

"What is it?" Billy asked, looking. "You see something?"

"I do not know, amigo, but I think I saw something up there." He pointed into the thicket.

Billy strained to look, then noticed a movement. "Everybody in the house, quick!"

Paolo looked at him, puzzled.

"Senor, get into the house," Billy said, drawing his gun.

Suddenly, shots were fired and Paolo crumpled. Billy ran to him. "Somebody give me a hand here."

Two ranch hands came to his aid, picking up the bleeding Paolo and rushing for the house.

Shots came from everywhere then, and another ranch hand fell.

Finally, they all found sanction in the house. Consuelo frantically looked after Paolo as Billy took up a position at a window and shouted orders to the others. A fusillade of bullets began tearing through the house. Wall paintings danced, chips of adobe cascaded around the room, and lanterns shattered.

Billy cursed and fired rapidly. When he ran out of bullets, he looked around. "Give me that rifle quick," he shouted to the cook. Taking the rifle, he pitched his six-gun to the man. "You reload, and be quick about it."

He glanced at Paolo, who lay still on the table. Consuelo was weeping. Then he turned and continued firing.

Cotton ran forward, sliding under a cattle trough. He resumed firing. Beelow sought the sanctity of a stable. Rusty attempted to hide behind a tree not wide enough for his bulk and the fusillade of bullets forced him to seek another vantage point.

A slug passed close by Billy's head, causing him to duck instinctively, but rose up again immediately. He was angry to be holed up like a cornered rabbit.

"Billy," Chavez shouted over the roar, "the patron's dead."

Billy heard but had no time to stop at the moment.

"Keep shooting, men," he shouted as broken glass showered him. "If they rush us, we don't stand a chance." He handed the cook his empty rifle and took his handgun, now loaded.

Chavez, reacting quickly, rushed to a broken window and fired just as Beelow looked around the stable door. The slug caught him squarely in the chest and he staggered out and fell.

One of the firing ranch hands yelled and grabbed his shoulder. He sat down, grimacing, and Consuelo ran to help him.

Rusty was hit in the knee and he fell screaming.

A bullet whizzed by Pete. Turning, he saw other rider's approaching. He looked around quickly. Beelow was on the ground, dead, and Rusty was nearby, holding his wounded knee.

Pete shouting above the din. "Fellas, let's move out. There's too many of them. Let's go!"

Bob, Cotton and Clint sprinted back up the hill towards their waiting horses. Bullets cut a path on their heels as they disappeared.

"Hey, men," Billy shouted, "we've got them on the run." He ran outside and fired until the gun was empty. It was then he looked and saw Harry Two-Horse with a small posse. He was tired, and shaking as he sat down.

Chavez walked up to Rusty just as he tried to grab his gun, only to have it kicked out of his reach.

"This fight for you is over, hombre," Chavez remarked.

Harry reined up. "We heard the shooting and got here just in time. Anybody hurt?"

"Paolo's dead, Harry," Billy said, looking up, "and we got several wounded. You seen Elliot?"

"No, we haven't. He should be here before long. He went after Maria."

"Is Rafer with him?"

"Rafer's dead, amigo," Harry said in a low voice. "We are going after the others now." Turning his horse, he shouted, "Let's go."

Billy sauntered over to Chavez, who was holding the wounded man at gunpoint. "I know you from Las Cruces, don't I?"

The man looked up in pain and grimacing, said, "Got a cigarette? At least I got the son-of-a-bitch that killed my brother. That Stewart bastard won't be coming back."

"Wanna bet?" Billy said, smirking.

At that moment, Consuelo walked between Billy and Chavez. Billy was shocked to see this gentle creature holding a rifle awkwardly. The bandit looked at her in horror. She pulled the trigger and the rifle jumped in her hand. The man rolled over, dead.

Looking down at the body, Billy said, "Well, Chavez, let's look after the wounded."

An hour later, Elliot brought the buckboard to a stop at the ranch. Signs of a terrible gun battle were everywhere. As he helped Maria down, they saw a weeping Consuelo walk up.

"Consuelo, what has happened? Where's my father?" Maria cried.

Consuelo gestured toward the house. Maria ran toward the door as Billy walked up to Elliot.

"A few of them got away, Elliot. We did the best we could, but they snuck up on us and the first shots killed Paolo," Billy said sorrowfully.

Elliot was stunned. Then, thinking of Maria, he raced into the house and saw Paolo lying on the table with a blanket over him. Maria was kneeling beside him, softly crying. Elliot approached, putting his hand on her shoulder. Paolo had a peaceful look on his face. For a brief moment, Elliot stood there, then his face hardened and he turned. As he hurried for the door, Maria said, "Elliot?"

He turned and looked at her.

"Kill the men that did this to my father."

He nodded and continued.

Billy met him outside as Elliot went to saddle Toter. "I'm going with you this time, Elliot," he said, "it's my war, too."

Bodine and his men rode into Las Cruces. Tying their horses at the hitch rail, they hastily entered Mason's Bar.

"You fellas wait out here," Bodine said. "I'll be back in a minute." He entered Sonny's office unannounced.

Sonny, working on his books, took his spectacles off. "Well, did everything work out?" he asked.

"Let me put it this way, Mason," Bodine explained. "Paolo's dead and so are about eight of his hands. With the girl gone to Mexico, seems to me you ought to walk in and take over, easy."

"'Paolo's dead, you say? What about the posse that left out of here yesterday ~ and guess who was leading them, Elliot Stewart."

"Hell, I thought he was dead. It don't matter now. We want to get paid and leave this place."

Sonny went to the door and peered into the bar. "I only see three of your boys out there. Where's the rest of them?"

"Dead or captured, I don't know for sure. So, how about our money?"

"Seems to me, you ain't finished yet," Sonny remarked.

"Look," Pete said, angrily, "we done what you wanted. Most of the cowhands are dead or run off. The girl is on her way to Mexico, and her father's dead. You been sitting here doing nothing. Now, you can clean up the rest of what's left. We want our money."

Sonny hesitated, then went to the safe, spun the combination, and extracted a handful of bills. He began counting. "Let's see, five hundred for each of you boys, that's fifteen hundred ..."

"Hold it, Mason, there were seven, not counting me. Better start counting again," Bodine said calmly.

"But Bodine, four of them are dead. They can't use the money," Sonny declared.

"Don't matter. I started out with seven, and they helped with the job. Besides, that Aragon fella paid you five thousand in cash," Bodine said irritably.

"Huh?"

"Thought I didn't know about that, did you? Do you take me for a fool? I figure you owe me seven thousand," Bodine said, glancing out the window.

You're crazy, Bodine," Sonny said nervously. "I ain't got that kind of money."

Bodine whipped out his pistol and hit Sonny across the head. Sonny fell hard to the floor, unconscious.

Bodine gathered the fallen bills then looked in the safe and took what remained. No sense leaving any of it, he thought, because Sonny ain't stupid enough to complain to the deputy. Stuffing the bills inside his shirt, he calmly walked out.

"Let's go, boys," he declared.

"Aw, c'mon, Pete," Clint said, "let's have a drink. I'm dry as a bone."

Pete momentarily stopped at the bar.

"Gimme a bottle, barkeep," he said.

The bartender put one on the counter.

"Charge this to Mason." Tossing the bottle to Clint, he said, "Satisfied? Now, let's move it."

"Sheriff," deputy Trent said, panting heavily, as he burst into Tom's room. "I just saw Bodine and three of his men leave Mason's bar."

"You saw Bodine?" he pondered, "and only three of his men? Wonder what happened to the rest of them? The posse must've caught up with them. Here, Foster, give me my pants." He threw off the covers and rose. He grunted as he struggled into his pants and boots.

"What are you gonna do, Tom?" Trent asked.

"I know that all hell is busting loose, and I ain't going to be caught in bed for sure," Tom answered, coughing and holding his chest.

Slowly, they walked out into the street just as the posse rode in. Tom hailed them down and was appalled to hear of Paolo's death. He informed Harry that Bodine had just left town, heading north with three of his men.

Harry rallied his men and they continued on Bodine's trail.

Tom and the deputy entered Mason's Bar. "Mason in?" Tom inquired.

"Yeah, sheriff, but he don't want to be disturbed," the barkeep said, wiping the bar. Ignoring him, Tom knocked on the office door, then burst in. Sonny was sitting in a chair, holding a bar towel against his bleeding head. Tom noticed the safe was wide open, papers scattered everywhere.

"What do you want here, Tom?" Sonny said, snarling.

"Wiped you out, didn't he?" Tom said.

"I don't know what the hell you're talking about."

"Sonny, you're a damned fool," Tom said. "You had it all, but you got greedy, didn't you? Couldn't leave things well enough alone, could you? Now, Paolo's dead and his people are on a rampage and I don't blame them. When the posse catches up to Bodine, he's history, and when Elliot returns, I wouldn't be in your shoes for all the money in the world. Did you think that you could deal with the likes of Bodine and come out ahead, huh?" Disgusted, he turned to leave. "Let's go, Foster."

Shortly after the lawmen left, Jenny appeared carrying boxes of recent purchases at the general store. Seeing Sonny hurt and the safe opened, she dropped the packages.

"What happened, Sonny?"

"It was Bodine. He came in demanding a lot more money than was coming to him. Then he pistol-whipped me and took it all."

"What do you mean, he took it all?"

"I mean, dammit, he took all the money that was in the safe. He cleaned us out. We're broke and we've got to leave town."

"You mean you got to leave town, you wimpish fop. I'm not going anywhere," she said, angrily gathering the fallen parcels. "I warned you about taking on the Lazy P outfit, didn't I, but no, you never listen to me. Now you've paid for your stupidity, and you want me to go with you? Ha, that's a laugh. You run, and I'll keep the bar."

"You're my wife," he shouted, "and if I go, you go. You hear me?"

She hurled a package at him and spat in his face. Enraged, he jumped up and struck her hard across her face. As she fell backward, her head hit the sharp corner of the safe door.

"Jenny, honey, I'm sorry," Sonny said, kneeling beside her. Cradling her head, he brought back a bloody hand. As he stared in horror, he noticed a pool of blood seeping from beneath her red tresses.

Arriving in Las Cruces later, Elliot and Billy headed for the sheriff's office. Tom and Foster were standing outside as if waiting for them. Tom informed them that Harry and the others had headed north, chasing the remnants of Bodine's gang.

Elliot looked over at Mason's Bar. "Is Sonny still here?" he asked.

"Yeah, but Jenny's dead. It was an accident, Elliot. They had a fight."

"Well, I can't say I'd want to shed any tears over that woman," Elliot remarked. "Well, I'll deal with Sonny later. We need to catch up to Harry."

"Elliot, you can save some time by going through the Alamogordo pass over the Sacramento Range," Tom said. "It's tough going, but you can pick up at least an hour."

"Thanks, we'll do that. Let's ride, Billy."

By nightfall, after taking the shortcut, the two came into the small village of Alamogordo. They were bone weary, but stopped long enough to ask if the posse had passed through. They were informed that the men had come through not a half-hour earlier.

Soon after leaving town, they came across the posse, who were camping for the night. Hot coffee and cooked beans greeted them. Elliot had forgotten that he was famished. They sat and talked as Elliot wolfed down his supper. When they had finished, Harry gave them a bottle of tequila. It was cold that night and the tequila was warming. One of the posse members approached them.

"Hey, fellas, with Mr. Paolo dead, who's gonna pay us to keep riding?"

Elliot, with the bottle in his left hand, jumped up and started to hit the man, then thought better of it and let his arms fall to his sides.

"Easy, partner, easy," Billy said, calming him.

Elliot turned to Harry. "Get rid of them, Harry. Get rid of them all. We don't need them."

"He's right, Harry." Billy added. "We can handle it from now on."

"Okay, if you want it that way," Harry said, and turning to the townsfolk, he told them to return to Las Cruces in the morning. He would see that they got paid for their trouble.

Elliot sat back down, took a long drink, and stared into the mesmerizing fire.

"You know, Elliot," Billy said, "it was a dirty shame that Paolo was killed. He was a good man, a real gentlemen."

"Yeah, everything was going our way. I mean for me and Rafe. We finally found a good job working for a good man and now look at it. Rafe's gone and so is Paolo. There's no damned justice out here in this godforsaken wilderness," Elliot said, wiping his eyes. "That damned Mason got greedy. He's behind every bit of this, and when we run down Bodine and his killers, I'm going after him. Jenny's death don't change nothing."

Billy spat into the fire, nodding his head.

"What say we get some sleep, boys," Harry said. "We got a long way to go tomorrow."

Elliot corked the bottle and laid it aside. It was bitter cold, and he, among others, slept as close to the fire as possible.

20

Early the next day, the three of them watched as the other posse members left, then they continued north. The trail was easy to follow for Harry, although it began to snow.

That night, they ate sparingly because in their haste to pursue Bodine's gang, they had neglected provisions. Vengeance had driven Elliot to the point of exhaustion.

The next morning they came upon a group of friendly Apaches and traded for a little dried buffalo jerky. Harry asked, in Spanish, if they had seen any sign of the desperados and they answered affirmatively, pointing in a northeasterly direction.

Later, Harry dismounted and surveyed the relatively fresh tracks in the snow. Cautioning the others that they were close, he walked his pony forward. He stopped and breathed in.

"I smell smoke, amigos," he said.

Topping a slight rise, they looked down. Nestled against a hill was a single room adobe cabin. A wisp of smoke was rising out of the rock chimney. There was a small corral to the right of the cabin containing five horses. Beyond that was a small lean-to.

"There's no back door," Harry whispered, "and one small window. If we can cover the front, they are trapped."

They ducked instinctively when the door opened and an Indian woman emerged carrying a wooden pail. A man followed her, kicking her backside. She stumbled forward to obtain water. The man stopped and looked in their direction, but evidently not discerning any movement, continued following the squaw,

"Look to the right of the cabin," Elliot whispered. "There's a man lying there. He looks dead."

"Probably is," Harry said. "That's his cabin and his woman."

"Let's split up," Billy said.

"Sounds good, amigo," Harry agreed. "Elliot, you and me need to get closer." He pointed down and to the left. "Billy, you keep the high ground and cover the door." Billy nodded, cocking his rifle.

The woman, filling the pail, went back in the cabin. The man patted her on the backside as the door shut behind them.

Elliot and Harry crawled down the slope, taking up positions together. They did not have to wait long before the door opened again and another man, with startling white hair, appeared carrying a rifle. He looked around and started toward the corral. A shot came from Billy's rifle, hitting him in the foot. The white-haired man screamed and fell down, crawling toward the corral. He turned and started shooting, but not knowing exactly where his adversaries were, his shots went wild. Billy rechambered a bullet and shot again. This slug caught him in the shoulder. He cursed and yelled for his attacker to stand up and show himself like a man.

"No shots from the cabin yet," Harry said. "They can't see us."

Almost immediately, shots were fired from the window, trying to draw fire from above, but it didn't work. The white-haired man was screaming for help while firing blindly. Billy, mad because he had not drawn a finer bead, leveled his rifle again. He held his breath as he slowly squeezed the trigger. A second later, the man jerked back as the slug found its lethal mark.

Silence descended for a brief moment.

"Elliot, see the chimney. I can move around to the rear, climb on top, and stop it up. We can smoke them out," Harry said.

"Okay, Harry, you do that and I'll give you cover." Harry, stooping low, ran around to the left. Spotting him, the cabin occupants began firing, as did Elliot. Finally, Harry, out of eyesight, approached the cabin and climbed above it. He jumped down on the roof, took off his parka, and stuffed it into the chimney opening. The cabin rapidly filled with smoke. He waved to Elliot.

They got to come out now, Elliot thought, his gun cocked.

The door opened and another man rushed out but before Elliot could react, he turned and shot Harry. Harry grabbed his arm and fell backward on the roof.

Elliot and Billy shot simultaneously, and the bandit spun around and fell.

Smoke was pouring out of the cabin now, partially obscuring the premises. Elliot recognized Pete Bodine, who bolted out of the door, and with bullets kicking up snow all around him, vaulted over the corral rails.

Grabbing a pinto's reins, Pete jumped on his back, and spurring his horse vigorously, slammed into the rails. The rails scattered and his horse leaped over. In frustration, Billy emptied his rifle at the fleeing desperado, but Pete escaped unscathed.

Rushing out of the cabin, the last Bodine, Clint, blinded by the smoke, shouted, "Pete, don't leave me! Pete, where are you?" While wiping his eyes, he waved his pistol around defiantly. Elliot was shocked by what happened next. The Indian squaw appeared, coming out of the cabin and brandishing an axe. She raised it high over her head and struck Clint in the back. He screamed and fell forward. She raised the axe again, but seeing that Clint was dead, threw it aside. Calmly, she walked over to where her man had fallen

Elliot rushed toward the cabin just as Harry rose up, and walking to the roof edge, jumped down.

"Harry, you hit bad?" Elliot shouted, panting heavily.

"No, amigo, I am all right," Harry responded, "but I'm freezing to death."

Elliot walked over to one of the dead men and removed his heavy parka.

"Let's wrap up that arm first," Elliot said.

Billy came down the hill, leading the horses.

"Hey, fellas," Billy said, "that last one got away. He was moving so fast, I never could draw a good bead on him."

"Don't worry about it, Billy," Elliot said. "Bodine's mine anyway."

Billy walked among the slain bandits. "God, almighty," he yelled, "look at all the greenbacks these fellas were toting."

"That's got to be Mason money," Elliot said. 'Take it. They got no more use for it anyway, but give some to that Indian over there. She could use it."

Finishing working on Harry's arm, Elliot said, "Well, that should hold you until you get back to the ranch."

They mounted up to leave.

"Billy, tell Maria that I will deal with Pete Bodine and then take care of Sonny Mason before I come back to the ranch. It will take a few days, so tell her not to worry," Elliot said, turning his pony.

As he rode toward Roswell, he thought of Rafer lying in a pool of blood, and the killing of the gentle Paolo. He would avenge their deaths if he had to ride to the ends of the earth.

The darkness, however, forced him to rest for a while. He didn't bother to build a fire, even though it was near freezing. He sat against a pine tree and pulled his hat down over his face, then folding his arms inside his thin blanket, tried to sleep. He did not notice the soft snowflakes falling.

At daylight, he was on the trail again, and the higher he climbed, the colder it got. Thankfully the snow had ceased. For two days he continued, and finally, he reached a pass that descended on the east side of the mountains.

Bodine's trail led directly to a small ranch at the foot of the hills. Rising up in his saddle, he surveyed the layout.

There was a small, single room adobe shack and a lean-to and a split-rail corral. Looking closer, he spotted a saddleless pinto in the enclosure. Could he have been so lucky to have caught up with Bodine so soon?

A short, stoop-shouldered man exited the shack, walking toward the lean-to. Elliot cautiously rode around the area and approached the lean-to on the blind side of the shack.

The man looked up, and possessing a toothless grin, greeted him. "Howdy stranger."

"Howdy," Elliot responded. "Say, where's the man that owns that pinto yonder?"

"Mister, I own that animal. Do you want to buy him?"

"No, but I'm interested in the man that did own him," Elliot said.

"Well, the horse is spent and the man traded him for a fresh one," the man revealed.

"So, he's gone then?" Elliot asked.

"Yep, he's on his way to Roswell, I suppose. Leastwise he's headed in that direction. Why, you know him?"

"Well yes, and he owes me," Elliot lied.

"If he owes you, mister, you might collect, cause he's carrying a bankroll of money. I seen it."

Elliot paused long enough to roll a cigarette.

"Can I have one of them?" the man said. "I ain't had a smoke in weeks."

Elliot tossed him the pouch. "Keep it. By the way, what kind of horse is he riding now?" Elliot said, lighting his cigarette.

"He's a big roan," the man replied, "and got a white mark on his nose. Why don't you get down and set a spell. I don't get much company way out here."

"Sorry mister, no time, but thanks. I ain't never been in these parts before. How far is it to Roswell?"

"Oh, about forty miles in that direction," the man said, pointing northeast.

Elliot wheeled his mare and bade the man farewell.

Three days in the saddle brought Elliot to the outskirts of Roswell. There was no sheriffs office to be seen as he made his way slowly down the dirt street. Looking from side to side, he could not see a roan with a white nose. He cursed his luck. I'll find him, he thought, no matter how long it takes.

Elliot made his way to the only tonsorial parlor to be seen. While getting a shave, he asked the proprietor about Bodine. "Yeah, I know Bodine sure enough," the proprietor answered, "but why are you asking? You a friend of his?"

"Hardly," Elliot replied, but it was too late to be cautious and he was tired. "He came to the ranch I was working on down Las Cruces way and shot up the place. So I'm here to settle the score."

The proprietor stepped back momentarily to size Elliot up. "Don't surprise me at all, mister. He's a real bad one. Got most of the folks hereabouts buffaloed and they ain't got much use for him. You'll be doing all of us a favor if you got rid of him. Better understand me, he's a known back shooter, so watch yourself."

"I understand, mister. Now, where can I find him?"

"He's got a shack about two miles north of here, but when he's here he plays poker almost every night over at Pearl's whiskey parlor," he said, pointing his straight razor. "See it over there just across the street?"

Elliot nodded.

"Fine," he said. "Now where can I go to get some rest?"

"Well, hell, mister, you can use that cot there. Nobody will disturb you, and I'm getting ready to draw the shades and close up anyway."

Elliot took a hot bath and started to lie down.

"Listen, you rest and I'll clean up the place. You want me to wake you?" the proprietor asked.

"Yeah, in about an hour," Elliot replied, taking off his boots and gun belt. As soon as he laid back, he was asleep.

Shaking him, the proprietor called, "Wake up, mister, it's dark outside and I need to leave."

Elliot sat up abruptly, trying to shake the fog from his brain. "Oh, yeah, thanks." He slowly turned in the cot, sat up, and put on his boots and gun belt.

"Pearl's, you said, eh?"

"Uh, huh, and mister, good luck."

Elliot paid the man and stepped out on the street. Checking his colt, Elliot reseated it gently in his holster. He stretched his fingers and walked toward Pearl's place. The establishment was dimly lit as kerosene lamps gave it an eerie, ominous glow. Elliot, stood inside the door a moment so that his eyes were well adjusted to the light conditions and then stepped forward. He felt a bit uneasy, but knew that it was normal for anyone about to face danger, yet Rafer's death drove him. Glancing around, he did not see anyone that fit Bodine's description, but recalling the barber saying that Bodine played poker, he spied four men dealing at a corner table. He obtained a drink at the bar, then turned and slowly walked over to the table.

The players all looked up at him, then continued playing.

"Want to join in, stranger?" one of the players said a moment later.

"Don't mind if I do, fellas," Elliot replied, reaching in his pocket for some money and sitting.

He played loosely, losing a few hands, but his mind was not on the game. At one point, he threw in a hand that clearly was a winner. About an hour later, a man strode in, and seeing him, Elliot pulled his hat down lower, hiding his face.

"Psst, mister," one of the players whispered, "you better move over. You're sitting in Bodine's place."

"I am, huh," Elliot whispered casually, not moving.

Bodine obtained a bottle and a glass from the bar and walked over.

"Hey, you," he demanded, "do you mind moving over a mite? That's where I sit."

Slowly, Elliot stood up, cocked his hat back, and looked directly into Bodine's eyes.

Looking him up and down, Bodine said, "Don't I know you from someplace?"

"Yeah, Bodine, I'm Stewart," Elliot replied.

Eyes widening, Bodine dropped the bottle and the glass and reached for his pistol. He was fast, but Elliot's gun was faster. The deafening roar resounded throughout the small bar as the patrons scattered. Bodine looked down at the hole in his chest. Reflex action did prompt him to pull the trigger, but as he was a standing dead man, the bullet shattered harmlessly into the floor.

Bodine fell and dust rose as his body slammed onto the floor.

Elliot looked around, but nobody moved. Then he holstered his weapon and started for the door.

"Hey, mister," the bartender said, "What am I supposed to do with this mess you left here?"

At that moment, the barber walked in. "Don't worry about it, John," he said, "I'll clean it up." He turned to Elliot. "Thanks, mister, I had to watch."

Elliot turned and walked out.

Riding into Las Cruces, Elliot looked over at Mason's Bar and stopped his horse. Mason's was no longer there. Only blackened remains greeted him. Puzzled, he rode over to the sheriffs office and walked in.

Sheriff Gentry, seeing him, stood up and extended his hand.

"Elliot, it's good to see you again. We heard what happened about Bodine's gang, but what about Bodine?"

"Bodine's dead," he said. "But what happened to Mason's place, and where's Sonny?"

"Oh, he's outside," Tom said casually. "C'mon, I'll show you." He led Elliot out on the sidewalk and pointed at a man sitting against the building. "There he is."

Elliot walked up and stood over a dirty, disheveled man who looked up at him with blank, bloodshot eyes. It did not resemble the Sonny that Elliot had known. He had an unkempt beard and spittle emitted from the corners of his mouth.

"What happened to him?" Elliot asked, frowning at the sight.

"Well, after Jenny's death, we all expected Sonny to hightail it out of town. When we started to remove her body, he came up with a gun and told me and Foster to stay away. Anyway, later, he set fire to his place with Jenny still in it. He just stood outside and watched it burn. As you can see, he's a dummy now," Tom explained. "You've won."

Elliot looked at him. "I ain't won nothing, sheriff. I lost my closest friend and Senor Paolo, all because that man there got greedy. Well, what's done is done."

"I guess it's over now, huh?" Tom asked.

"Yeah, it's over," Elliot said, sighing. Grabbing the reins of his horse, he mounted, and taking a last look at the bowed, shaking head of Sonny, he turned for the Lazy P.

Elliot, nearing the ranch house noticed the remaining hands moving about. Billy and Chavez greeted him as he hitched his horse. Consuelo, sweeping the lanai, dropped the broom and ran into the house. In a moment, Maria emerged.

Slowly, Elliot approached her as she stared at him longingly. She reached up and kissed him softly.

"Maria, I'm sorry that your father will never get to see his grandchildren," he whispered.

"He will, my sweet, he will," she said, leading him into the house.

THE END